GUATEMALAN
RHAPSODY

GUATEMALAN RHAPSODY

Stories

JARED LEMUS

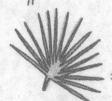

ecco

An Imprint of HarperCollins*Publishers*

GUATEMALAN RHAPSODY. Copyright © 2025 by Jared Lemus. All rights reserved. Printed in the United States of America. No part of this book may be used or reproduced in any manner whatsoever without written permission except in the case of brief quotations embodied in critical articles and reviews. For information, address HarperCollins Publishers, 195 Broadway, New York, NY 10007.

Portions of this work were previously published in different form in the following publications: "So Long to the Rearview" originally appeared in Issue 14 (Summer 2022) of *Story*; "Saint Dismas" was originally published in *The Atlantic*, online on March 9, 2024, and in the April 2024 issue; "Caídas" was originally published online in the Fall 2024 issue of *The Kenyon Review*; "Whistle While You Work" was originally published in Issue 43 (Spring 2022) of *The Pinch Journal*.

HarperCollins books may be purchased for educational, business, or sales promotional use. For information, please email the Special Markets Department at SPsales@harpercollins.com.

Ecco® and HarperCollins® are trademarks of HarperCollins Publishers.

FIRST EDITION

Designed by Alison Bloomer
Title page art by Vivian Rowe

Library of Congress Cataloging-in-Publication Data
has been applied for.

ISBN 978-0-06-338164-3

24 25 26 27 28 LBC 5 4 3 2 1

For Taylor, Jack, and Felix,
always *y para siempre*

And for all the *chapínes, aquí, allá, o donde sea*

Contents

OFRENDAS 1

SO LONG TO THE REARVIEW 23

WHISTLE WHILE YOU WORK 37

SAINT DISMAS 55

HEART SLEEVES 75

CAÍDAS 95

BUS STOP BABY 113

FIGHT SOUNDS 129

SCRIMMAGES 149

HOTEL OF THE GODS 169

DARK ROAD WITH DIESEL STAINS 189

A CLEANSING 209

ACKNOWLEDGMENTS 227

GUATEMALAN RHAPSODY

OFRENDAS

The old bring the clothes of their sick, the young bring cigars and cigarettes. Women bring ropes, sugar, and chickens; some want protection for their children, others against having children, then there are those who ask for protection from their children. The men bring scarves, hats, and *aguardiente*; they ask for love, for money, for a good harvest. Each of these petitions represented by a candle—white, yellow, red, and even a few black—the wax melting onto the ground with prayers that curse enemies, call for infliction of pain on past lovers, invoke death. Some couples ask for cleansings before marriage, others for visions of their future together. People bring chocolate and sugar to appease—this is the most subtle ask: please, show me favor. Some seek guidance and bring incense to help their prayers float up to the ears of the gods; others seek attention or help and give *quetzales* or salt. There is so much want in this world, and it is up to the *sajarins* to help fulfill requests; today is no different—the temple is full of petitioners, and it is the healer's duty to serve, much like the priest in the Catholic church, as a conduit between the people and the ears of San Simón.

Yuma, metal rod in hand, is seated in front of the firepit he has built. A woman, mid-thirties, sits across from him, their eyes shut in prayer. Yuma mutters a few final words of thanks, then stands. He bangs his staff against the ground— once, twice, thrice—and calls for Cabaguil, Kinich Ahau, and Vukubcane to hear the woman's requests. Finally, he walks around to her and helps her stand. The woman opens her eyes long enough to hand Yuma the egg that she's brought. Yuma takes it and runs it over her head and chest, her shoulders and legs, down to her feet, all while praying. He then places the egg in the fire and tells the woman to watch. They both stare, the heat emanating from the pit causing sweat to drip down their foreheads. It takes a few moments, but the egg finally cracks.

"A yes," Yuma says, and the woman lets out a small sigh.

She bows her head a little. "Thank you," she says. She swipes at her eyes with the back of her hand, then kneels down to pick up the bag of sugar she brought with her. She looks around in search of her son. "He must still be at the altar," she says.

Yuma nods, then motions for her to follow him. They walk past other *sajarins* tending fires—six rows of pits, eight pits per row with just enough space between one flame and the next for people to walk by single file, all of the fires surrounded by sugar or salt. Some of the sajarins have symbols of the god or gods they are attempting to contact drawn in chalk on the asphalt in front of the steps leading up to the *cofradía*. Others use staffs to pound on the steps to garner the attention of the divine, then fill their mouths with rose water or alcohol that they spit onto their petitioners. Yuma and the woman take one stair at a time, bypassing other sajarins who slap branches against people's bodies to rid their souls of bad thoughts and evil spirits.

Inside, the *cofradía* looks like a gutted monastery—no pews, no bibles, only people whose eyes burn from the smoke of cigars and cigarettes brought forth as offerings and placed in San Simón's mouth. The smoke wafts upward, is so thick, the petitioners struggle to make out the 120-centimeter-tall San Simón figure carved from tz'ite' wood sitting on the low table that serves as his altar. He is surrounded by tiny statues of his likeness left as tributes and candles of all colors. Two *sajarins* stand beside the statue, the one on the left—Hermano Zumez, twenty-four, the son of the former leader of the *cofradía*—taps the remaining ash from the cigarette in San Simón's mouth into a jar and seals it; the one on the right— hermano Xavier, thirty-one, a recovering alcoholic saved by San Simón—removes the cigarette butt and places it in a different container, both of which will be sold: the ash for luck and to cure insomnia, the butts to ward off thieves.

The next person with an offering steps forward and hands a 100-millileter bottle of *aguardiente* to Zumez, who uncaps the bottle while Xavier tips the statue backward, so that the slits carved in the wood as eyes look up at the ceiling. Zumez pours half the bottle into San Simón's mouth, where a tube funnels the liquid down through the body and into a container hidden below the figure so that the liquid can be rebottled and resold to other petitioners. And even though the *cofradía* is full, it is reverentially quiet and the alcohol sounds like a river. Zumez then recaps the bottle of *aguardiente* and holds it out to the man, who tells Zumez to keep it as an offering. Zumez nods and sets the bottle on the table next to the other quarter pints and candles.

Now the woman's son steps forward and produces from his pocket a folded bill. Xavier motions for him to step closer. The boy does and places the money on the altar next to dried, hardened candle wax. And though he doesn't say aloud what he is asking for, his mother knows that he is asking for a second chance.

AT THE END of the day, once the gates are closed to the public, four of the *sajarins* take San Simón to a back room in the *cofradía*, where they remove his clothes and the medicine bundle at the center of his being, as well as the heart—the essence of San Simón, which can be seen and touched only by blessed members of the *cofradía*. They lay him down to sleep and hand the clothes to Yuma, whose job it is to take that days' layers of silken shirts down to the lake, where he will wash each article—including the many scarves wrapped around San Simón's neck as offerings—and bottle the water for healing ceremonies.

Yuma makes the trek down the steep path to the lake, using his staff for balance. It is dark, and the owls can be heard in the trees. The only light comes from the candles in the *cofradía* up the hill, the stars, and the bulbs of the nearby town across the lake. Yuma kneels to collect a pail of water. He lays San Simón's clothes on a smooth boulder and begins washing them with his hands, stopping every now and then to massage his knuckles—swollen from years of scrubbing. His back hurts from leaning over the garments, and his feet feel like pumice.

When he is done, he squeezes the water out of the clothing and bottles it, then hangs each item up to dry. Finished, he sits down to rest before starting the trip back up to the *cofradía*. His knees sound like *matracas*, and he hopes the spirits don't confuse the sound with a summoning. He chuckles at the thought; and this should be the only human sound, but then he hears a splash in the water. Yuma angles his body toward the noise. There are no fish in the lake and it is too late for anyone to be swimming. Yuma stares out, but the lake seems placid. He waits for another splash, but it doesn't come. Instead, he hears someone walking down the path. Yuma turns but can make out only their outline, which seems too small to be that of one of the brothers of the *cofradía*.

"State your business," Yuma calls out.

The silhouette pauses, as if also shocked to find someone else out this late at night. The shape turns to run, but Yuma calls out again, telling it to stop. The outline freezes in place, then, in a small voice, it says, "Please don't tell my mom."

Yuma reaches for his staff and stands, then summons the voice forward until the shadow turns into the face of the boy who came by with his mother earlier.

"You've returned," Yuma says, then scans the jungle and the makeshift path behind the boy. He turns toward the lights coming from the other side of the lake. Nothing but darkness between the two places.

The boy, as if reading Yuma's mind, points up to the road beyond the temple's courtyard and says, "I rode my bike."

Yuma nods. The potholes in the road, the snakes waiting in the brush, the kilometers between here and town, the dark.

"¿What is it that brings you back without your mother's knowledge?" Yuma asks.

The boy tries to look at his feet, but Yuma leans forward and uses his staff to lift the boy's face to his until the boy can't take the stare any longer.

"I wanted to know if San Simón would answer my prayer," he says.

Yuma straightens up, listens to the water lap at the shore behind him. "¿And what is it you've asked of him?" Yuma asks.

The boy looks at the water over Yuma's shoulder, then down at the rocks by his feet.

"Very well," Yuma says, then stoops to pick up the jars of water he's bottled. He places some in his pockets and holds the rest, and without another glance at the child, begins his ascent to the *cofradía*. After a few steps, Yuma hears the boy's feet shuffling behind him.

"I asked for more life," the boy says.

Yuma stops, then turns to face him, evaluates him. "¿How old are you?" he asks.

The boy shakes his head. "It's not for me," he says.

Yuma can see tears in the boy's eyes. He reminds him of himself at his age, back when he was lost and looking for direction. Yuma feels a breeze coming from across the lake, and even though he's wearing a bandana, the wind sweeps up the strands of his hair that hang down his back.

Yuma sighs. "I am not supposed to do this after the gates have closed," he says, then sets down the jars he's carrying in his hands. Yuma sits on one of the stones used as steps that lead up to the *cofradía* and wipes away the sand with his sleeve. He reaches under his shirt, up near his heart, and pulls out a red satin pouch the size of his palm that he keeps in a small pocket sewn into the inside of his shirt. The opening of the bag is threaded with a yellow string that ties it shut to keep the sacred stones, black beans, red beans, and other small objects he has found during his spiritual journeys into the mountains from falling out. He found it—his *grandesa*—during his first spiritual quest into the mountains, when he'd spent three days without food or water, praying to San Simón to guide him to a medicine bundle belonging to any former *sajarin* who knew his end was near and had hidden his *grandesa* to be found by another worthy healer and fortune teller. Yuma had sworn he would find the bundle or die in those mountains and had, on the third night, been led by moonlight to the hiding place of the pouch he now holds in his hands, the *grandesa* from which all of a *sajarin*'s powers are derived.

Yuma motions for the boy to join him on the steps. The boy approaches cautiously, reverentially, and Yuma can hear howler monkeys—naturally diurnal animals that should be sleeping—waking as if the sun has risen, calling out to one another in the canopy. The boy sits across from Yuma, one leg on top of the other, like an infinity sign.

"¿Did you bring an offering?" Yuma asks. The boy shakes his head, and Yuma nods. "Close your eyes," Yuma says, and the boy does as he's told. Yuma begins his prayer to the gods, and up here, the gods listen. Yuma praises, which is pleasing to the gods. He thanks, which the gods receive with open arms. Yuma promises offerings—sugar and chocolate—which he does not have with him but will give to them in the morning. This does not sit well with the gods, but they will hear his petition before deciding whether or not they will answer.

Yuma reaches into the sacred bag—the hole just wide enough for his hand, the edges fraying from the constant opening and closing—and pulls out a handful of stones and blessed items. He lets them drop back into the bag one at a time until he is left with one—an answer. Yuma opens his eyes and instructs the boy to do the same. In his closed palm he holds what the boy came back for. Yuma opens his hand, and at the center of it sits one black stone.

Yuma drops it back into the bag.

"¿What did they say?" the boy asks.

Yuma ties the *grandesa* closed and places it back near his heart. He stands, using his staff for balance.

The boy stands, too. "¿Did they say yes?" the boy asks. His hands are clasped in front of his chest.

Yuma leans over to collect the jars at his feet but is struggling to grasp the last one. The boy scoops it up, the water sloshing inside, and hands it to Yuma, who takes it and turns from the boy. Yuma takes a step toward the *cofradía*, then another. "Go home," he calls to the boy. "It's not the answer you want."

The boy follows after Yuma. "Wait," he says, but Yuma doesn't. "¡Stop!" the boy shouts. He reaches down and picks up a pebble, then throws it at Yuma, missing his head by a few centimeters. Yuma finally halts and turns. "Maybe you read it wrong," the boy says. His eyebrows are pulled down toward the center of his nose, his fists clenched at his side.

Yuma glares at the boy.

"All I mean is," the boy says, he looks at his surroundings as though they have the answer, "it's dark, and I didn't have an offering. Maybe they weren't happy with that."

Yuma is still observing the boy—his hands and brow have returned to normal, but there is still heat radiating from his body. Yuma knows this will go nowhere, so he nods. "Go home," he says again, "before your mother worries."

The boy, as if remembering where he is for the first time, gasps, eyes wide, and runs past Yuma back up to the courtyard, where he must jump over the gate or slip through the bars to get out. Yuma listens as the bicycle's oxidized chain—a film of patina from rain and mud covering the surface—clicks into place and begins to spin faster and faster, the boy's breath lost in the night, as ephemeral as a prayer.

THE NEXT DAY, the boy is there again. Yuma has done his morning chores and is walking out of the *cofradía*, down the front steps to his firepit, where he will talk with petitioners and interpret for San Simón, when he spots the child in the crowd, behind the bars of the still-locked gates that lead into the courtyard. It doesn't seem to matter to the boy that there are others in line ahead of him, because the moment the latch is unlocked, the boy is the first one inside, weaving through the other bodies, running the thirty meters between him and Yuma in a matter of seconds.

Echoing his tactics for dealing with the crowd, the boy skips all pleasantries: no good morning, no thank you for your help last night, nothing. He stands about chest-high to Yuma and says, "I need your help changing their minds."

Yuma glances over his shoulder at Hermano Zumez and Hermano Xavier, who are both watching his interaction with the boy from the top step of the *cofradía*. What will they think of the boy's imprudence and of his familiarity with Yuma? Will they recognize him as the child who stepped forward with a monetary offering yesterday or will they await an explanation at the end of the day? Yuma decides that is for him to deal with later. For now, he has a petitioner in front of him and a line of them not far behind.

Yuma looks into the unlit firepit. "¿Did you bring an offering?" he asks.

The boy nods and pulls sugar from his pocket, no bag, just loose granules. He reaches into the other pocket and pulls out somewhat-melted pieces of chocolate. "I have cigarettes and candles in my socks."

Yuma doesn't ask where the cigarettes came from and can't imagine them having held their structural integrity as the kid's feet sweated on his bike ride here. "¿What's your name?" Yuma asks. The kid, short, with dark-brown hair, undernourished, about twelve years old, looks into Yuma's eyes—the same dried-mud color as his own—and says, "Ikal."

Yuma nods, tells Ikal his name, then looks the boy over once more. "Before the offerings," Yuma says, "a cleansing." He motions for Ikal to follow him next to the steps leading up to the *cofradía*, where he picks a branch from one of the sacred bushes that have been blessed by the *hermanos*. He then has Ikal follow him into the temple, where he grabs a bottle of rose water. "¿Do you have a donation?" Yuma asks. The boy reaches into his pocket for the chocolate. "Not that," Yuma says. "Money." Ikal looks at the ground. "Very well," Yuma says. He reaches into his pocket for a few coins and hands them to Ikal, then motions for him to hand them back. "Follow me," Yuma says and leads the boy back down to the firepit.

Yuma uncaps the glass container, the size of a miniature perfume bottle, and places the cork next to his feet. Yuma closes his eyes and begins his prayer. When he is done, he takes a swig of the rose water and keeps it in his mouth. He uses the branch, patting at Ikal's face, then spits some of the rose water onto it.

The moment the water lands on the boy's lips and forehead, he opens his eyes wide in shock. "¿What the hell are you doing?" Ikal shouts. He wipes the droplets with his shirt collar. Others, including some of the *hermanos*, have turned to look. "¿Do you think that's funny?" Ikal says. His brows are pulled together, just like they had been the night before, but his palms are open at his sides and he uses them to shove Yuma hard enough to drop him to the ground. This is the first time he and the boy have made physical contact, and it is like a lightning strike to the chest, where the boy has pushed him.

Yuma's eyes roll to white, and suddenly Yuma is no longer Yuma; he is Ikal a week ago. He is Ikal on his way home from school, books hanging from a rope tied to the handlebars of his bicycle. He is Ikal when the boys—four of them, each on his own bike—stop in front of him and prevent him from passing. He is Ikal as they shove him to the ground and ask if his mother has sex for money now that his father is gone. He is Ikal when they ask how much she charges, when they ask if they can have a turn and grab at the zippers of their pants. He is Ikal with dirt on his hands and blood running down his knees and onto his lips; Yuma is this boy who has shoved him to the ground as he picks up a rock the size of a *pan dulce* and brings it down against the skull of the oldest boy in the group, he is him as he brings it down again, harder than the first time. He is Ikal as the other boys pull him off, is still him as he watches the blood mix with the dirt on the ground.

When Yuma is Yuma again, he is on his back staring at the blue above. His tailbone hurts and the back of his head feels heavy. He blinks, and the boy—Ikal—appears above him, knee pressed into Yuma's chest, punching away, until he is pulled off by two of the *hermanos*. Two other *sajarins* help Yuma to his feet. Upright, Yuma sees that the boy is being brusquely escorted to the gates, sugar and melting pieces of chocolate spilling from his out-turned pockets. Yuma can hear the boy apologizing but can't speak up for them to let him go, to tell Ikal what he's seen. He watches as the brothers point Ikal in the direction of town, watches as the boy picks up his bicycle just beyond the gates. Yuma blinks, and the boy is gone. He blinks again, and . . .

WHEN HE WAKES a few hours later, Yuma finds that his head has been bandaged and that there is a throbbing in his lower back. He sits up in his bed and listens as the springs sing in relief. He positions himself so that he can get his feet on the floor, one at a time, then lets his head hang between his knees.

The vision he'd had plays vividly in his mind's eye. Ikal— bullied to the point of retribution—and the boy bleeding at Ikal's feet. What Yuma hadn't seen was how Ikal, after the other three boys had ridden off to pretend nothing had happened, had gotten on his bike and pedaled to the nearest corner store to beg for help. He didn't see how Ikal had asked for the boy's mother's name and directions to her house, how he'd ridden there faster than he'd ever rode before to let her know what he had done and where to find her child.

Yuma tries to stand and ends up in a sitting position again. He reaches for his staff and manages to pull himself up from the bed. His legs tremble as they adjust to the weight of his body, but he is soon able to take his first step. He uses the wall for support and opens the door to his room—the same as all the others: space enough for one twin-size mattress and bedframe, one bedside table, and nothing else. He follows the barren walls, past the other rooms, through the kitchen, and into the main sanctuary, where worshippers are gathered at the altar of San Simón. It is high noon, Yuma can tell by the smell of cloves—the scent of the incense lit before lunch prayers. One of the brothers notices him and approaches.

"You should be in bed," he says. "We will take care of your duties." Yuma can tell the brother is angered by this, that he's been told to say this by Xavier or Zumez.

Yuma tries to wave him away, but the brother does not let up. "If you have lost your abilities as a servant of the temple of San

Simón," he whispers while holding Yuma's sleeve at the elbow, "find a mountain and give up your *grandesa*." The brother points west, adjacent from the town, where ten kilometers away, are mountains—including the one where Yuma found his medicine bundle all those years ago.

Yuma pulls away from the *hermano* and leans on his staff as he makes his way to the front door without glancing back. He walks, slowly, down the steps and past the firepits to the front gate, where he locates a tuk-tuk driver willing to take him up to the town in exchange for a reading he says he doesn't believe in.

It isn't until he has finished the driver's reading that Yuma realizes he doesn't know how he's going to find Ikal. He walks the streets hopelessly, his back hurting, his hips aching, until he gives up and decides to find a place to rest. Yuma leans against a tree in the center of town and people begin to take notice—his clothes, his staff, the long hair. A few pedestrians, regular visitors to the temple of San Simón, stop and ask if he needs help.

"Ikal" is all he can say. "¿Do you know him?"

People shake their heads, bring him water in paper cups, and leave sweet breads by his legs in case he gets hungry. Yuma leans his head against the tree and closes his eyes. Soon, the rumors begin: a *sajarin* on a pilgrimage, too old to make it to the mountains; a disgraced *sajarin*, kicked out of the *cofradía*; a drunk who's dressed himself to look like a *sajarin*—scarves around his neck, one tied around his waist, the Maya Pantheon stitched onto the cuffs and collar of his shirt, and a wig. It doesn't take long for the whispers to make it to Ikal by way of adults talking around nosy teens, who then lord the information over the younger kids—all bored out of their minds, in search of a story, even a false one.

When Ikal hears the rumor of a *sajarin* ghost walking the streets calling out the names of children he must take back with him, Ikal knows it's Yuma. Ikal jumps on his bike and rides to the town center, weaving in and out of traffic on his fixed gear, passing street vendors, avoiding dogs, and jumping over empty beer bottles along the way. By the time he finds Yuma sitting under the tree, bandana pulled down over his eyebrows, he is winded. "¿Yuma?" Ikal says.

Yuma begins to stir and slowly opens his eyes. He makes out Ikal's face, the sweat dripping from his forehead down to his nose. Yuma pushes his bandana back onto his head. "You killed him," Yuma says. He looks into Ikal's eyes, the sun setting behind him. "You're just a boy." Ikal doesn't reply; instead, he reaches for Yuma and helps him up from his slouched position. "Your soul will be forever marked," Yuma says, groaning as Ikal helps him sit up straight. He feels like his back is made of reeds, all cracking under the weight of his own body.

Ikal finally speaks. "Drink some water," he says, raising one of the paper cups surrounding Yuma. But Yuma turns his head away, refuses the water. Ikal sighs loudly, then crumples the cup in his fist. Water drips down his forearm until he throws the cup into the street. He sits down next to Yuma, knees pulled up to his chest, forehead pressed against them.

Yuma coughs, his head vibrating like a gong. "That anger," he says, "it got me into trouble, too."

Ikal turns his face toward Yuma, only one eye visible. The cars driving by honk at one another, friends greet each other with kisses on the cheek, *eloteros* walk the narrow alleys.

"I made the same mistake as you," Yuma says. It's the first time he's spoken it aloud in almost forty years. "A long time ago."

Ikal turns to look at Yuma with both eyes now. "¿What happened?" he asks. Yuma doesn't answer, but Ikal can tell he's reliving the event in his memory. He waits, but Yuma stays silent.

In his head, Yuma remembers what Ikal can't know, won't ever know: that Yuma had been twenty-five and lost. His parents had kicked him out of their house when, at sixteen, he announced himself to be an atheist. He spent the next few years being homeless, sleeping inside only when he could afford a room or convince someone to sleep with him. It was during one of those nights that an ex-husband had shown up at the door of the woman with whom Yuma was in bed.

What could have been avoided turned into an altercation when Yuma claimed the man's ex-wife had never been satisfied by his meager cock. It wasn't Yuma's first fight. In fact, he'd been in more fights than he could remember. The ex-husband swung, and the rest is still a blur in Yuma's mind—a hit to the body, a few to the face, a final swing that knocked the man to his knees, followed by a kick and the sound of a skull bouncing off the concrete floor.

Yuma ran away that night and spent the next five years blind drunk, drifting from town to town avoiding the police and working as a day laborer on coffee plantations or as a plow-hand in the fields. One day, he awoke in the middle of the *cofradía*, still reeking of booze, unsure of how he'd gotten there. It was then, by accident or by fate, Yuma can't say, that the rest of his life began. The brothers had welcomed him with open arms, saying that San Simón never makes mistakes. And, sure enough, Yuma had eventually felt the calling of the *sajarin*, trekked into the mountains, and found his *grandesa*. He'd gone from a self-proclaimed denier of all deities to someone who thanked San Simón every day. Thanked him every day for granting him a second chance.

Yuma begins to cough some more, bringing him back from his thoughts.

Ikal leans over and picks up another cup of water left behind by a concerned stranger, offers it to Yuma. This time Yuma accepts. Ikal holds the cup to Yuma's lips and studies his weathered face, the wrinkles that look like the waves made by boats on the lake, the pockmarks like volcanic craters. Yuma drinks; his chest hurts, and he wonders if the boy pushed him hard enough to break his ribs, or if he has what he's heard referred to as "internal bleeding."

"The sun is setting," Yuma says as Ikal puts the cup down beside him. Yuma tries to stretch his back, but it catches and spasms. He lets out a small yelp, like a dog that's been kicked, then settles back against the tree.

Ikal reaches over to wipe a droplet of water from Yuma's face, but Yuma pushes his hand away and dries his chin himself, then closes his eyes again.

Ikal frowns. "I wasn't going to hurt you."

Yuma nods, eyes still closed.

"And he's not dead," Ikal says.

Yuma opens one eye, slowly, and looks over at Ikal. "¿Who isn't?" he asks.

"The boy I hit," Ikal says. "Tanio. He's not dead yet."

Yuma feels his heart begin to beat against the *grandesa* next to his chest. "¿Yet?"

Ikal nods.

"¿How do you know?"

"I visited him every day," Ikal says. "But he's getting worse, and his mom won't let me into the room to see him anymore." Ikal looks away, and Yuma can see tears forming in his eyes. "I have to watch him from outside the window," Ikal says. He wipes his tears with his shirt collar.

Yuma listens to all this. The boy—Tanio—is still alive. "There's still time then," he says, reaching for his staff. He strains against the pain in his head, his back, and his chest, and stands, Ikal jumping up to help.

"¿What are you doing?" Ikal asks.

Yuma huffs out a breath, then inhales sharply. "I need Tanio's clothes," he says.

Ikal doesn't think he's understood correctly. "¿His clothes?" Yuma nods.

"Okay," Ikal says, thinking. "I can probably go to his house. I know where he lives. I can sneak in if I have to."

Yuma holds up his hand. "No," he says, "I need the clothes he had on when you hurt him."

Ikal flinches, as if he's been slapped. "I didn't mean to," he says, but Yuma puts his hand up again.

"Bring me the clothes stained with the blood that spilled from his head," he says, using his staff for balance. "Bring it to the *cofradía*."

Ikal nods, and Yuma watches him as he hops on his bike and waits for an opening to cross the road. Yuma begins to murmur a prayer as Ikal weaves through traffic to the curb on the other side. Yuma prays, then tugs on his shirt collar and reaches into his *grandesa*, watching Ikal as he turns down an adjacent street. Yuma finishes his prayer, then pulls out one stone to see the answer. Ikal has disappeared around the corner. Yuma places the stone back in his bag and closes it.

BY THE TIME Yuma makes it back to the temple, the sun has set and the gate has been closed. The brothers will have had dinner after laying San Simón down to rest. Someone will have been sent to wash his clothes in Yuma's stead. Yuma reaches into his pocket and pulls out a key, quietly unlocks the bolt to the gate, and makes his way to his firepit. The brothers will, of course, notice, but hopefully not until it's too late.

Yuma begins by using the metal rod, as quietly as possible, to connect his pit to the one next to it. He brings coals and kindling to bridge the gap. Once he's done, he begins the process again until he's connected six pits to form a rectangle in the center of the courtyard. He is pouring salt around the perimeter of what he has built, when he hears Ikal's bike and labored breathing coming down the dirt road. Ikal throws down his bicycle and runs through the gates, sweat dripping down his arms and onto the ground.

"Quiet," Yuma says. He points at the entrance of the *cofradía*.

Ikal nods, then reaches into his backpack and pulls out a shirt with dried bloodstains around the neckline and shoulder seams, a tear down the lower back.

"¿You did that?" Yuma asks, using his staff to point at the hole. It was not something he'd seen in his vision.

Ikal shakes his head. "His mom was there" is all Ikal says. What he doesn't say and what Yuma can't know is that Tanio's mom had been asleep on a cot next to his bed when Ikal snuck through the window. Ikal hadn't noticed her at first, had walked around in the dark, checking under the bed and under the chairs to no avail and had finally almost stepped on her when he crossed the room. That's when he saw it—there, under Tanio's mom's head, a makeshift pillow, a plastic bag filled with Tanio's clothes. But the moment he tried to pull the bag, Tanio's mom shot up and started shouting at him to let it go. She yelled for a nurse, a doctor. Then the bag ripped and Tanio's clothes fell to the ground. They both reached for them, Tanio's mom quicker, taking the pants, but they both had a hold on the shirt. "¡I'm trying to save your son!" Ikal shouted, but the mom wouldn't listen. "Your voodoo magic won't help him," she said. "Only God can save him." But Ikal knew that wasn't true. He'd been brought up Catholic. Hadn't stopped believing until the year before when he prayed his father wouldn't leave, but he still did. He wanted to say this to Tanio's mom, but that's when the nurses ran into the room and Ikal did the only thing he could think of—he kicked Tanio's mom with all his strength and climbed back out the window before the nurses could figure out what was happening.

Yuma looks at the hole in the shirt again. "¿Are they coming?"

Ikal shrugs his shoulders and shakes his head at the same time, his mouth hanging open. "I don't know."

"Quickly then," Yuma says, pointing at a sack of candles— all black—next to all the other supplies he has collected and snuck out of the *cofradía*.

Ikal takes a step toward them but then notices the giant pit. He stops. "My mom said healings are done with water." She had friends who'd been coming to the temple for years, had followed their advice to bring Ikal to the *sajarins* after the accident.

Yuma nods, proud of Ikal's knowledge. "But we are also asking for forgiveness." He points at the candles again and motions for Ikal to begin setting them up around the pit that he's built.

Ikal hesitates for a moment, unsure of why they need a pit so large. He looks around, remembers the story of Isaac and Abraham and wonders if there's a goat trapped in the bushes somewhere or if the pit is for him.

"Hurry," Yuma says, too forcefully, and begins coughing. He clutches at his ribs and looks over at the *cofradía*, but no lights have come on yet. Ikal rushes over to the bag full of candles, lights one, and begins placing the others around the pit, keeping them upright using hot wax from the one he's lit. Yuma grabs the pitcher of oil he's prepared and limps around the coals, drizzling a trail behind Ikal.

"Light the rest," Yuma says, handing Ikal the box of matches. As Ikal begins the process, Yuma crumples to the floor. He feels as if his head is melting. He removes his bandana, soaked with what he thinks is sweat. Then he removes the bandage the brothers tied around his head and sees that it's wet with blood. Ikal is working his way back down the other side, so Yuma quickly hides the wrappings in his pocket.

Ikal stands next to Yuma, who sits on the ground, once all the candles have been lit. "¿Now what?"

Yuma reaches for him, and Ikal takes a step back. Yuma looks into his eyes and shakes his head. "Come," he says.

Ikal takes another step back, but Yuma motions for him to stop. "Come," he says again. It takes a moment—Yuma can see the deliberation in Ikal's eyes—but then he does as Yuma says and approaches, slowly. Yuma extends a hand, asking for help. Once on his feet, using Ikal for balance, Yuma says, "When I light the fire, the brothers will come. They may try to stop me."

Ikal shifts under Yuma's weight. "¿From doing what?"

Yuma tries to respond but wheezes instead, bone pressing into his lungs. He reaches into his pocket and pulls out an egg he sets next to the pit. "For after," he says, then pushes away from Ikal and stoops down to grab a tinder bundle. He takes the matches from Ikal and begins setting the coals aflame. The fire spreads and grows tall. Yuma and Ikal watch as it reaches its full potential. Yuma turns to say something to Ikal, but the doors to the *cofradía* open and the brothers step out, still half asleep.

"¿What is it you're doing, Yuma?" Xavier calls from the top of the stairs. "It is after hours."

"Bring up water from the lake," Zumez directs. Some of the *hermanos* run back inside for pails before rushing down the hill.

Yuma turns to Ikal and knows he must act fast. He lays both hands on Ikal's shoulders. "There hasn't been a human sacrifice since before the Spaniards," Yuma says. Ikal turns to run, but Yuma holds him with all the strength he has left. Ikal's eyes are filled with tears as he faces Yuma again. Yuma wipes them away with his thumbs, places his hands back on Ikal's shoulders, and remembers the question Ikal's mother had asked Yuma the day he met her, when she brought sugar and asked him to build a fire: "¿Can his soul be saved?"

Yuma pulls the boy close. He recalls what it was like for him when he killed that woman's ex-husband. Yuma hears the brothers shouting as they make their way back up the path with the pails of water. "I have hidden my *grandesa*," he says. He doesn't have time to explain, so he places his hand over the boy's eyes and gives him a vision. The one of him leaving the town square earlier that evening, when he'd found a tuk-tuk driver, promised him everything in the offering box at the *cofradía* and all he'd saved if the driver would take him to the base of the mountain and wait for him to come back. The one where Yuma went as far as he could and finally found a tree with a hole in its center, where he'd said one last prayer before reaching in and leaving his *grandesa*.

They come out of the vision as a car pulls up in front of the entrance to the courtyard with its headlights shining brightly into the faces of everyone inside the gates. Tanio's mom and a nurse step out and take in the scene before them.

"If you feel the calling," Yuma says, "you know where it is." He lets go of the boy, gives him one final nod, then steps into the fire, where the flames begin licking at his heels and calves. But Yuma doesn't make a sound. He lays down supine, eyes staring at the smoke as it rises toward the sky.

The brothers with the pails of water have made it to the first row of pits but are stopped by Xavier and Zumez, who realize what Yuma has just done—not just a prayer, a sacrifice. They instruct the brothers to drop the water and run inside for the *matraca* and staffs. Tanio's mom runs to Ikal's side and looks into the fire, where Yuma lays motionless, eyes now closed. She places a hand on Ikal's shoulder as the brothers begin banging their staffs against the ground, calling for the gods to listen, begging for favor, asking them to accept this offering. They begin to walk around the perimeter of the rectangle that Yuma built, each of them in vocal prayer.

Ikal, with the *hermanos* walking around him in a circle, stoops down to pick up the egg Yuma left for them and hands it to Tanio's mom.

She looks at it, confused. "¿What do I do with this?"

Ikal, still a boy, places his hands over hers and says, "Ask a question."

The mom looks at him, sees his sincerity, his remorse. Finally, almost ashamed for doing so, she whispers a question that only she and Ikal can hear and hands the egg back to him. Ikal nods and stoops down to place the egg in the fire, the flames licking at his wrist and hand. They watch and hold their breath. They wait and they wait and they wait.

SO LONG TO THE REARVIEW

The next curve is a tricky one. Too much pressure on the gas and the van could tip. Not enough, and the truck a cigarette-length from your fender will send you flying cliffside. Or worse, overtake you round the blind corner. This happens, and your regulars will click their tongues, say each second costs them money. You check the rearview with the crack across its length and missing top-left corner. Do a quick head count. About equal per side, but the heavier ones are on the right. Plus, cargo weight up top won't help. Gonna have to do your best to make sure all four wheels stay on the ground. You tap the accelerator and turn the steering wheel, let the downhill force do the rest. Someone calls from the back. It's their stop up here. Francisco leans out doorway; no need to roll down window or open door. Gone. Removed for efficiency. Francisco signals at the truck behind you that you're pulling over. The van door in back slides open and Don Juarez and his pregnant wife climb out.

Moment Francisco has their fare, your wheels are spitting rocks and dirt as you swing back onto the asphalt. You've been up since before the roosters and got six hours of sunlight left.

Up ahead, you see someone flagging you down. You start to slow, but when you get close, you see it's Hector—gold teeth shining like a beacon. You double tap the gas and he's *adiós* in the rearview. Francisco is giving him the bird, and you can't see Hector through the dust, but you're sure he's doing the same.

"Fucking asshole," Francisco says, sitting down in his seat. He pulls his cowboy hat back on. Learned his lesson 'bout leaving it on when leaning out the doorway.

"And broke," you say.

Last time you picked up Hector, he stiffed you on the fare. Always that chance with him. But the van is full today. No rain yet, and people are out. No need to risk it. A motorcycle zooms by on one wheel. The woman on the back, baby over her shoulder, leans into the driver's neck. The baby looks at you. Is wrapped so tight it can't move. Then they're gone, down the hill, and you're pulling over to let someone else out. Then back on the road.

Behind your seat, a woman counts beads, prays for safety. Francisco rolls his eyes, tells her to shut up. He's young. Late twenties. Likes to act older. But he's a good worker, so you keep him. Helped you out of a few bad situations once or twice. Like the time the van did tip over, years ago. No one died, barely a wet eye from the passengers. He hooked you up with a mechanic who gave you a discount, so long as you agreed to transport the occasional sack of marijuana when needed. Now you get paid to do it. No one knows what's in the bags, or that they belong to you. It's easy enough. Got one up top right now, as a matter of fact.

Another stop, and Francisco climbs up the back, unstraps a sack, and tosses it down to a boy no older than yours is right now. The boy hands over money and is gone faster than Francisco can count.

"¡Hey!" Francisco calls.

"Let him go," you say.

"It's five short," Francisco says.

Ten per head, five per passenger bag.

"Chase him, then," you say.

Francisco looks in the direction the boy went. You look, too. Nothing but trees.

"Son of a bitch," Francisco says. He hops back in the van. "Any of you motherfuckers tries that," he says, loud enough to be heard in the back. He taps his machete against the dash.

"¿Someone need to get off here instead?" he says.

The heads in the rearview are all shakes.

"Good," Francisco says.

He slaps the side of the van, and you're off.

YOU REACH QUENOTEPEGUE. No one on board but you and Francisco.

"¿Gonna drop now?"

You check your watch. Ten minutes early, and you can make it back to Sacopiquapan without gassin'. Shift to first and up the streets narrow as gauge needles. Vendors approach, mangoes, *agua de jamaica*, *horchata* in hand. They peek in back, leave to find another van. You buy a pack of *nueces*, an orange Fanta, an *hamburguesa*, all without stopping. Up ahead, the chop shop. Pocket the keys. Francisco already out.

"¿Macón?" Francisco says.

The man with the tire iron, face black from car grease, jerks his head toward the back. *Gracias* and through the door. Macón, shorter than you, doesn't look happy to see you.

"But I got the merch," you say.

"Didn't ask for it. Not my problem." Walks by you to another car and peers at the engine.

"But you always want it."

"Not this time." Something about money, a falling-out, and that you have to take it up with *el jefe*, and then he leads you out.

"Don't come back," he calls and waves goodbye.

In the van, Francisco is itching, slides his hand down the leather sheath of the machete almost sensually. He's never used it. Likes to pretend he would if needed. Now what? Trip back with smoke still strapped to the top?

"Just the fingers," Francisco says.

You don't say nothing back. Imagine what he'd do if you said yes. Piss his pants or tell his mom, then you'd never see him again. Not worth the pain of finding someone new. You tug on your shirt, sent down from someplace up north. Tighter than a year ago. Mustard stain from the burger on a logo you don't know. Lick at it and pull it back down over the spare tire round your midsection.

"Can't go back with this," you say.

Francisco's eyes follow the invisible line shooting from your finger. Thieves. Or worse: cops. Or worser: thieving cops. You risked enough traveling the eighty-two kilometers one way, not to mention back and uphill with the slowness of *por favor* rob me. No. You'll take it to Sávvie's. Maybe stay for five minutes up front begging for a pit stop, a quick in and out, then five minutes with your pants around your ankles and her legs up on your shoulders. You check your watch, and it says the stop will cost you extra; can already hear passenger fares, that should be yours, jingling in someone else's pockets. Shove the key in and shift into first. No complaints from the van, smooth purring like it agrees.

"Buckle up," you say.

Francisco sighs, has heard that one too many times.

THE BRAKES SHRIEK outside her house, but no horn. Kid could be asleep. Or maybe he's at school. You and your passengers work seven days a week. It's a miracle you know the year, but the weekday is a mystery.

"Stay in the car," you say. But Francisco already knows. He's reclined his seat, cowboy hat over his face.

You step on a tire and untie the rope, swing the bag over your shoulder like Hispanic Santa. Except you deliver burdens. House door is white, but the walls are green. Only house on the block not red or blue or pink. Stands out like envy. Not covetous of neighbors. They got nothing, too. Covetous of those who don't have to be here.

You kick a now-empty bag of trash dragged here by a stray dog. Startle another with the sound. He growls, and you bark loud. You were an alpha once. Back before the end of your marriage with Coralina. Before the knee problems. Used to fuck wives and girlfriends up and down this street 'til the roosters went home. Got caught but wouldn't let Coralina kick you out. That's when she packed up and skipped town, moved to the capital. Took the boy, should be about nine years old now, with her. Don't got an address or list of friends. Gone *adiós*, and you: all alone now. Only Sávvie lets you keep coming round. You don't know why, but she likes you for some reason. And you let her think there is one.

One knock, then two, and one for good luck. Then wait until Sávvie, maybe two years older than Francisco, appears at the door.

"Fuck no," she says and tries to slam it shut. But your hand is like a mongoose—in through the crack before she can stop you.

"It's not what you think," you say.

"Drugs," she says.

"Okay," you say. It is what she thinks.

"I can't have that stinking up the house with Jalisco here," she says. "And my mom. You know she's sensitive to smells."

"Two days," you say. It's the same thing you'd said last time and then left it for over a week. You couldn't keep it at your place—the one with an old TV set, a bed with holes for sheets, and not much else. Not since Francisco had convinced you to try the product, even though you don't smoke, you drink. Asked how you could deliver without knowing what customers were receiving. Then you couldn't think straight, got paranoid. The cops were watching. Had to keep it elsewhere.

"I can't have it around Benicio," Sávvie says.

It's true. Homeboy took like an ounce, and Sávvie's been fucking you with more frequency to make you forget.

"¿You don't want me no more?" you say.

"It's not that," she says, crosses her arms to hide behind. "He asked," she says. "But I can't say yes until we're done."

It feels like a bus has landed on your chest. First Coralina, now this.

"¿You'd marry that asshole?" you ask.

"You don't even know him," she says and takes a step back. Then, "Get out." Then, "Now."

Homeboy's debt was paid off long time ago. You both know it. You and Sávvie had fucked before he took from the stash. He should have gotten it for free. Now she wants to go straight. And the one she's picked ain't you.

"Choose me instead," you say. You think you mean it. Could you quit this whole thing and move to the country? Live on what? Not that you have much to live on now.

"That's not who you are," she says.

"¿Who isn't who I am?" you say.

"A father."

The sack of weed on your back holds bricks and lead. You shift under its weight. Coralina, when she left, said you weren't a father to Isaiah. Hadn't acted like one. Hadn't stopped drinking—haven't stopped drinking. But it was more than that, she'd said. Your fingers smelled like women from the bar.

"Wants another baby but won't take care of the one at home," she'd told her friends.

"Not the baby he wants," they'd told her. "Just what the baby comes out of."

"¿Is homeboy a father?" you say. Sávvie's boy is almost two. Could conceivably be yours but isn't. You doubt it's boyfriend's either. Looks like *muchacho* who's always hanging round her front door when he sees someone come over. Smells like bread. Could work at the bakery or eat there a lot.

She doesn't answer, and you slam the door behind you. Bread boy is right outside, too. Same eyes and mouth as Sávvie's boy. Married, your ass. She's just tired of fucking you. You slap the windshield to wake up Francisco.

"Tie it up," you say, dropping the sack.

"¿We're taking it back?"

You don't answer, start the van. He can hurry up or ride up top.

Moment his foot is on the step, you take off.

"Fuck," Francisco says. Manages to climb in and sit down. "You almost left half of me back there."

"We're late," you say. But it don't matter no more. No way to make three more trips without driving at night. Can do only one more. Up until a few minutes ago, could have made two.

Come back and stayed with Sávvie. Now you got to end up back in Sacopiquapan or pay for a hotel out here in the place you used to call home four years ago when Coralina left.

Francisco holds his hand open to you. "Took some out of the bag," he says.

"Put that shit away," you say. "We're giving it all back."

"He won't notice," Francisco says.

"Customers will notice your eyes looking like Satan's asshole," you say.

This time Francisco laughs. "That's a good one," he says, and you hope Isaiah doesn't grow up to be anything like him. Anything like you. And maybe he won't. Not without you there to fuck it all up. Goddamn father of the year.

YOU'VE GOT TWELVE seats but twenty-six passengers. You're halfway back to Sacopiquapan when you have to pump the brakes. Up ahead, nothing but stopped cars. Line as long as the horizon. Worst part: no taillights. Engines are off. Get comfortable.

"¿Now this?" Francisco says, as though this is his bad day, not yours.

Groans from the back.

Guatemala is two-lane highway through its whole. Accident on one side, traffic for hours. Accident on both sides, fucked. No way round, no way through. Surrounded by jungle or cliffs or mountains. Stuck. And you here, homebound.

"Check the lanes," you say.

Francisco hops out to ask around.

Up ahead, a man has hung a hammock from side of his truck.

Francisco comes back. Collision. Semi versus motorcycle. Blind spot, overtaking, seventeen-year-old kid stuck under axles.

You shut off the engine. No AC anyway. Passengers exit, want to see the accident.

"We leave with or without you," you call after them, just in case they think you'll wait around. Some sit back down.

Soon, a boy—younger than yours, maybe four, maybe five—in back asks if he can pee.

Not your business.

The boy doesn't move. You check rearview, see him uncapping Gatorade bottle.

"¡Not in here!" you shout. Point at grass.

"My mom said to stay put," he says.

"Then hold it," you say.

"I can't," he says.

You see him in rearview. Squirming like *culebra*. Up front, man in hammock fans himself with cowboy hat. Fine.

Boy in front, you follow him into tall grass.

"¿Can you?" boy asks, shirt hem under chin. Fingers on button above fly.

"¿You can't?"

"Mom does," he says. Van will smell of piss, so you do. Then face away and unzip yours.

After, boy thanks you, runs ahead. You emerge from grass, and line is same length ahead and behind. You look at the sky. Sunshine is being replaced by rain due south and coming. Police drive by, no sirens. No emergency. You light your daily cigarette. Usually saved 'til after you're buzzed. Maybe you'll have two today. One per lost love.

Francisco has gone and come back with pictures, and do you want to see? No, but he is showing before you can say. News vans, coroner, no ambulance. Truck driver has survived, not a scratch. Family of boy in undercarriage asks for better roads. Francisco shows you recording.

"The highways are unsafe." A woman, business suit. "Accidents every day." She sobs into handkerchief.

You get it, toss your cigarette.

"I'ma show this around."

"Van also leaves without you."

He knows. Is over to next car with window down, asking do they want to see a video. You get back in driver's seat, look in rearview. Half are still at accident, other half snooze or sit while they can. Man in his hammock fans away.

WHEN YOU ALMOST turn back, engines begin to roar. You see lights, hear car doors close. Rain is less than two nose hairs from you, and passengers jump in. But where is Francisco? Side mirror. Objects closer than, so then why does he appear to be in slo-mo? He trips in and stares ahead, and you know. Eyes redder than taillights.

"Find another ride."

"I won't screw up the count," he says and extends a Bud Light.

You can smell him from here, but you can't do the job alone. Rearview says some would try to ride for free. Better him high than you counting both kilometers and fees. You snatch the beer. Feel all fifty-six eyes on your hand, crack the can like bruised knuckles. The liquid foams, then coats your chapped lips. Reminds you of the taste and feel of Sávvie. Smack, smack, and wipe with your forearm. Grass outside, same grass as last two hours, suddenly interesting to all inside when you shove key in the ignition.

Rain, so you flip switch for wipers. There's a click, but nothing moves. Blades remain in place. Francisco leans out and pulls. Now they're halfway up and stuck. Car ahead pulls up and others notice. Honk their horns to let you know. Cop cars drive by and one slows down, so you pull up. Squint through raindrops. Drive until you see car stopped not half a meter in front of you. Brake, and Francisco falls out. He climbs back in, and what the fuck? You're sorry, but you can't see shit. Car in front moves again and you follow. Slower this time. Too slow. You're up where accident is supposed to be. Not even an oil stain no more.

You tap the gas, then the other pedal. You don't trust yourself. Car horns grow louder. You hit accelerator again, but a car is trying to overtake you in the rain. You hear the scrape. Feel it drive up the car's side into your spine.

"Shit," you say. Look at Francisco.

See blurred brake lights. Then American is at your window. Accent gives him away. Younger than you. Skinnier, for sure. He has pulled your door open. He wants to see your license and exchange information. But you don't have any. None you're willing to give anyway.

You try to pull the door closed, but he is standing between it and the van. Rain still coming down. You tell him you have nothing to show, and he pulls out his cellphone. Asks passengers for emergency number, but no one says nothing. You try pulling up, but his car's in the way. And you cannot see. You remember what's up top just as he snaps, with flash, a picture of you with beer can in lap. He's on what he says is live video chat. That the cops will definitely see. You pull cowboy hat farther down face, but he insists it's too late.

"¿What do you want?" you say.

And he is adamant he wants your license and registration. He points at his Toyota and says it's rented.

He wants money. You look at Francisco, but he shakes his head. Moves his fanny pack closer to his doorway.

"They want me to take a bribe," kid says to phone. "Call the police."

No. Last thing you need. Cars float past, slow down to look, but none stop. Want no part. You attempt to close the door again, but kid doesn't move. Another car squeaks by. Stops. Driver rolls window down in rain.

"¿What is going on?"

"This guy hit my car," kid says.

"No, he ran into mine," you say.

A look from the driver. *Please*, your eyes say. *Please, I need some help.* A nod, and you think the man understands. But no, he's driving off.

The kid, you have his attention again, and he has something to say. He didn't buy the insurance, and cannot afford to pay for repairs out of pocket. You get out. He steps back, afraid. Phone is his only weapon. You look at damage. Nothing bad. Your headlight's *adiós*. Black scrape down side of his car. You don't know the cost, but you do know a mechanic.

"I don't want his help. I want your license and registration."

You can't give them. Can't afford this. Will get license taken. Maybe even jail if kid says intoxicated. Francisco is by your side now, machete by his. He's making things worse. Boy points phone at him.

"Look," you say. You can get all cash from passengers, but have nothing else.

"License," says kid, "and registration." Kid looks at Francisco. Studies his face like he knows him. "He's high," the kid says. Then he looks at you.

"He's not," you say. "We're not."

"But we do have weed," Francisco says. "A whole sack you can sell."

Cellphone light is bright in your face. Kid's mouth is wide open.

He got that on camera.

You want to say it's a joke, but man from car window is back. He didn't drive off. Was pulling over.

"I saw the whole thing," the man says. He also has phone out. Says he's a witness. "I saw him cut right in front of you."

It takes you a moment. Then you understand. He's come back to help you. This stranger, doing something your family would never.

"That's a lie," the kid says.

Another driver is beside you now. "¿What is going on?"

"This kid caused an accident," says first man.

Driver looks at kid, looks at you, sees Francisco. Man with phone points it at kid. And you can feel them—your eyes again. They're pleading.

Driver shrugs off rainwater. "I saw it, too," he says. He waves over to his car, to passenger side. "This kid crashed right into him. Tell the other drivers."

"That's not true," kid says. Holds phone out. "They're lying."

Others have come now. They circle around your van.

"¡It wasn't my fault!" kid shouts.

But they all disagree. Are shouting at kid to get out of the way. Cars begin to honk again, and you feel like you are being rescued.

Kid, for a moment, doesn't know what to say.

More and more of your people stand behind and beside you. It's like they're holding you up. You wonder if this is what it's like to be cared for.

Kid continues to shout. "¡This man is using you all!"

A woman older than you. "You should be ashamed," she says to the kid. "Having all of us out here taking care of this mess." A family of people who don't know you or your faults. They've come to protect you.

Kid begins to protest but then closes his mouth. Takes one final look at you and turns back to his car. He opens door, and engine turns over. Then you know you're *adiós* in his rearview.

You laugh and clap and breathe relief as crowd begins to disperse. You want to say thank you, but no one is listening. They are leaving, turning on headlights, driving by without another glance. They were helping themselves. Were tired of waiting. Would have said anything to get moving, out of the rain, out of the traffic, and home to their families. Then why were *you* in such a hurry?

"¿Should we go?" Francisco is standing next to you.

You turn to your van. Are soaked through to your soul. Inside, the little boy from earlier is waving, or wiping at window. You wave back, but then he is blowing warm breath. You realize there is no way he can see you. Not through the rain, the lights in the van that come from cellphone cameras. The boy draws a smiley face in the fog that he's made. You stand in the rain and watch it fade to *nada*. The boy does not care. He breathes again and draws another. And you here, surprised by how fast it disappears.

WHISTLE WHILE YOU WORK

The job started at five thirty in the morning. The crew was me, Jorge, and Shawna, and we were in charge of two buildings connected by an awning. The goal was to constantly look busy—emptying trash cans, mopping floors, and putting out WET FLOOR signs—while not working hard enough to finish all our duties too fast. The job sucked, but it didn't require a high school diploma, or even a GED, so I couldn't complain too much, I guess.

"Before you do the bathrooms in Fassler," Jorge called out to me from inside the janitor's closet, next to the table where we took our lunch breaks, "Shawna wants to see you." He emerged waving a communal walkie-talkie at me. I would only get one with my name taped on it after I passed what he and Shawna called the six-month free-trial period.

Shawna was the head custodian and the leader of the Ross Hall crew. She was older than me by over twenty years, and swore she'd been working as part of the janitorial staff since the day she was born. "Got a slap on the ass and a mop for my first birthday," she liked to say.

"Tell me it's not paint again," I said. It was too early to have to deal with scraping dried paint off the walls and then doing a fresh coat.

"Orange this time," Jorge said.

A few weeks earlier, I'd walked into a classroom on the fourth floor of Ross Hall to empty the trash cans and found one of the walls covered in blue paint. There wasn't a design or pattern, it just looked like someone had taken a paintbrush, dipped it into a can of paint, and then set about splattering it everywhere. Protecting the walls from any further non-university-sanctioned paint jobs had somehow become my responsibility.

"Where is it?" I asked.

"Said she'd meet you on the third floor," Jorge said, stretching like a cat in a La-Z-Boy rather than an employee on the job.

"You gonna take care of the bathrooms?" I asked.

"Yeah, man," Jorge said. "Easy-peasy, *y con una sonrisy.*"

That was his catchphrase. He'd told me that when he first started working there over eight years earlier, he and Shawna had a different crew leader. On one of the days the old crew leader and Jorge had to team up with the groundskeepers to chase a family of opossums out of the building, he'd asked Jorge where he was from.

"Mexico," Jorge said.

"Ever think you'd be hunting down opossums in America?" the man asked.

"No," Jorge said, adding that he was surprised by how often it happened.

The man told him the staff propped the doors open during the summer because the air-conditioning was spotty, and jokingly added that they should put opossum-corralling on the application as part of the job description.

"Hard work," Jorge said, crouching down by one of the traps he'd helped set up.

The man shook his head and told Jorge that when he was his age, he'd worked on a pig farm with his father. "Now, that was hard work," the man said. "This here," he said in his southern drawl, made worse by alcohol, "this here's easy-peasy, lemon squeezy."

Jorge had adopted the saying, giving it his own twist— easy-peasy, *y con una sonrisy*: easy-peasy, and with a smile. Ever since then, anytime Jorge had to do something he hated— cleaning up shit someone had smeared on the bathroom walls, re-mopping a hallway he'd just cleaned because a student dragged in mud, or shampooing the carpet in a classroom after someone brought in a dog with fleas—he'd repeat his stupid saying and remind himself and the rest of us that things could always be worse.

THE DOOR TO the room on the third floor where the paint had been spread—on two of the walls this time—had been blocked with three WET FLOOR signs, the closest thing we had to crime-scene tape.

"Fucking shitshow," Shawna said when I walked in. "You believe this?" she said, waving at the walls, almost not talking to me.

"I thought they were going to put in cameras?" I said.

According to Shawna, the school had been talking about upping their security for years. Every time there was an active shooter on the news, the plan was revamped, but nothing ever came of it. The same was true for getting door handles with key codes that would automatically lock after five minutes and for hiring overnight security guards to patrol each building, instead of only nine-to-fivers.

"Right after they give me that raise," Shawna said. She put her hands on her hips and let out a huge sigh. "Had to tell the chancellor," she said.

She'd told the chancellor's office the first time, too, and had received an email from the chancellor herself, asking how something like that could have happened on our watch, as if it was our responsibility to patrol the building after our shifts. In the email, the chancellor asked if we had any keys missing. Shawna had told her we were more careful than that, but the chancellor had sent someone from Lock and Key Services to account for all the keys in our possession anyway. When everything checked out, her office sent an apology in the form of two dozen donuts and a coffee for each of us, with a passive-aggressive note that read, "To keep the staff well-caffeinated and alert."

"Are you getting fired?" I asked.

"What? Hell no," Shawna said. "Day they fire me, the whole building'll collapse." She laughed. "No, this is worse," she said. "They want us to have our pictures taken so they can post 'em on the school website."

I didn't understand how that was the solution to the problem, but Shawna filled me in before I could ask, saying it was meant to put a face to the "real victims" of the crime. She'd caught the chancellor during her jog around campus, which she did at four thirty every morning. The chancellor had come up to the room, and within half an hour, her office had sent Shawna an email saying they'd contacted one of the freelance school photographers and that each of us was expected to show up in our best outfit the next day. She said we were also expected to talk with one of the school writers, who was going to ask us questions about our backgrounds and hobbies so he could write a blurb to go along with our pictures.

"All that before the banks are open?" I said.

Shawna shrugged. "Money don't keep hours," she said.

I nodded. "I don't have any hobbies," I said.

"Make something up," Shawana said. "Can't very well tell 'em you and Jorge spend your free time impersonating Cheech and Cheech," she said, laughing at her own joke. She turned to look at me. *Get it?* it seemed like she wanted to ask. *Because you're both Latino?* But she didn't. "All right," she said, signaling at the wall behind her. "Get to it."

THE NEXT DAY, Jorge showed up with an entire bottle of gel in his hair, and Shawna doubled over in laughter when she laid eyes on him.

"Better hope they don't use a flash," she said, and cackled all the way up to the sixth and final floor of the building, where they were going to take our pictures.

"Can you spell your first name for us?" the writer asked when it was my turn to sit in the chair. I could tell Jorge and Shawna wanted to stick around but also didn't want to appear not busy, so they'd left after their pictures.

"Santorío," I said, spelling it out. It was a strange name even in Guatemala, where my parents are from. I'd asked why they'd given me the name, since it wasn't a family name or anything, asked if it was like a male version of Santería, but they'd said it wasn't. It was a combination of the words *holy* and *river*, so only good things would flow into and out of me.

"Can you tell me a little about you?" the writer asked as the photographer instructed me to raise my chin a little and tilt my head to the right.

"I like to play guitar," I said, lying.

"What kinda guitar you have?" the writer asked, his pencil poised above his notepad.

I hadn't thought ahead that far, so I said nothing. Pretended I hadn't heard the question.

"How long have you been on staff?" the writer asked, moving on.

"Almost five months," I said.

"A young buck," the writer said to the photographer, slapping his knee with his notepad.

"Turn this way a little," the photographer said, pointing.

"Joined right after my twenty-third birthday," I said. The writer nodded and wrote this down.

"You like working here?" the writer asked.

The photographer pointed at his chin, instructing me to lift mine a little more.

"Hold it right there," he said, then pushed down on the shutter button.

THE BLURBS ABOUT us were up on the website later that week.

"Look at this," Jorge said, pulling up his picture. "That photographer made me look like a fat howler monkey." Jorge was in his early thirties, fairly light-skinned, had a slight accent, and was sensitive to every little change in his body, even though he did nothing to take care of it. He would come in to work sometimes and ask if we noticed anything different, and when we said we didn't, he would point at a new wrinkle or an extra pound, shocked by how it got there.

"You look the same to me," I said.

"Yours isn't any better," Jorge said, clicking over to my picture. It was true. The lighting wasn't great, but it was a work website, not a dating app.

"This part about your parents true?" Jorge asked.

It was. One of the questions the writer had asked me was why I was working as part of the "facilities management." I told him that I'd had to drop out of high school in my junior year after my parents were deported for having entered the country illegally, so I took the janitorial position because the university would pay for a GED course as part of my benefits package after I'd been a full-time employee for a year. I didn't mention that I was actually only two years old when my parents left me behind with my aunt, and that I'd dropped out to help her pay the bills, getting a job at a fast-food restaurant and staying on even after she, too, moved back home, unable to take the long hours working as a maid.

"That sucks, bro," Jorge said. "You still talk to them?"

Jorge and I got along, smoked weed after work most days, but we didn't talk about anything personal, so I kept it simple. Said I did, but that it was hard because of how expensive the calls were. I didn't tell him that my parents had to make a two-hour trek to the main part of town to use a phone, because they lived on a mountain in the highlands and didn't have one up there, nor that when I called, I lied to them, saying I worked at a college, which wasn't technically a lie, and that I had a girlfriend, that we lived in a nice place.

Shawna, who knew some of my story from what I'd told her during my interview and who had been sitting at the table behind us in the janitor's office, got up and glanced over our shoulders at the computer screen showing Jorge's picture. "Makes me *want* to deface private property," she said. Jorge tsked at her. "I didn't know you played guitar," she said to me, patting me on the back.

THE PICTURES DIDN'T stop the vandalism from happening again, so the school hired an overnight security guard for our building the following week. We met her during her orientation, when they brought her by on our ten a.m. lunch break. She was halfway between my height and Jorge's, tan, with an upturned nose and green eyes. I could tell Jorge wished he'd worn the hair gel that day. She introduced herself to each of us. "Courtney," she said.

"Will one of you show her to Lock and Key Services?" the head of security said to us, adding that someone had called out sick and that he had to get back to Weber Hall.

"I'll do it," Jorge said, nearly tipping his chair over.

"Aren't you on trash cans in Fassler?" Shawna said. "Santorío'll do it," she said.

Even if Jorge had wanted to protest, he knew better than to argue with Shawna. She'd put him on vomit and shit duty for the rest of the year if he said anything. With the matter settled, the head of security told Courtney to make her way back to the Security Services desk after she was done. She nodded, and we all headed down on the elevator.

"Pretty campus," Courtney said on our walk from Ross. I knew she was lying. The campus was made up of ten buildings, each spaced out almost a full block from the next, with no sports fields, no gym, and a library half the size of most of the ones I'd seen on TV.

"You new here?" I asked, then sneezed into the crook of my elbow. It was a nice day out—not a cloud for miles, but pollen like you wouldn't believe.

"No, I've lived here forever," she said. She couldn't have been older than me by more than a few minutes, but I knew what she meant; time in your hometown stretches like gum on a summer day.

"Why this job?" I asked.

"The discount," she said, explaining that campus security guards got a 60 percent discount on tuition. "Is it not the same for you?" she asked.

"Nah," I said, telling her I was technically part-time, since I worked only thirty-eight hours a week. "But they gave us donuts once," I said. She laughed, and I noticed that she had pretty teeth, all in a row, like small chalkboard erasers. We walked on quietly for a few seconds with students passing us on either side.

"So, someone's been painting the walls?" she asked.

"Yeah. Everyone's pissed." I tried to clear my throat, feeling like there were bees in it.

"I'll catch 'em," she said.

"Don't want to catch them too fast," I said.

"What?"

"Nothing," I said, and sneezed again. "They give you a gun or anything?"

"No, but I'll bring my own." She looked at me. "You should have seen your face," she said. I laughed, and I suddenly couldn't tell if I was sweating from the heat or from nervousness.

"Listen," I said once we were outside the Lock and Key Services building. "You smoke or anything?"

"I used to dabble," she said.

"Me and Jorge get together after work sometimes," I said.

"Well, now that I'm an officer of the law . . . ," she said, pointing at her laminated temporary badge. "But I'll think about it." She gave me her number and went inside. It was the first time I'd gotten a number in almost a year, and with it safely in my phone, the walk back to Ross Hall felt less stuffy. Almost like floating downriver.

MY APARTMENT WAS a one-bedroom with a bathroom so cramped, you could touch the sink, tub, and toilet at the same time if you wanted to.

"Place is smaller than I remember," Jorge said when we walked through the door.

"No discount here," I said, referring to his uncle, who was the super in his building.

Jorge splayed out on the secondhand couch I'd gotten from my aunt four years earlier, tossing one of the end pillows on the floor with his foot.

"At least take off your shoes," I said. He kicked them off. I went into the kitchen and checked the fridge for beer. I had most of a six-pack of PBR but not much food—a jug of expired milk I was still using for my cereal in the morning, some cheese slices, jelly, and leftovers from takeout I'd gotten the week before. I checked the cabinets and found only ramen and boxed mac and cheese.

"Got the munchies or something?" Jorge called from the living room.

"Should we order something for when Courtney gets here?" I said.

We'd been at Jorge's apartment smoking a bowl when I'd told him what happened with Courtney. Not believing me, he'd dared me to text her. I was high, so I did, and before I knew it, she'd agreed to stop by after her orientation. But one look around Jorge's apartment with his dirty dishes piled up in the sink, the two bags full of trash next to the can that had trash sticking out of it, and a carpet that looked like he owned a pack of stray wolves told me it wasn't the ideal location for a good first impression.

"You got delivery-fee money?" Jorge asked.

"We could pick it up," I said. "We got a couple hours before she's off."

"You go," Jorge said, taking out his wallet and handing me some bills. "*I'm* going to take a nap." I was exhausted, too, but I tried not to sleep until bedtime; otherwise, it took me forever to fall asleep and then I overslept the next day, and Shawna did not like tardiness.

I grabbed my car keys and picked up some cheap pizzas—including a cheese one, in case Courtney was a vegetarian—and a cheap bottle of rum, then woke up Jorge when I got back. We sipped on rum and Cokes and puffed on joints until Courtney got there.

"Neat place," she said, taking her shoes off as she walked in. I closed the door behind her and got her a beer and a plate. I noticed that she'd changed out of her uniform and was in jeans and a loose-fitting top.

"Hey," Jorge said, sounding like a drunk infant. "We were watching . . . ," he said, trailing off, looking at the TV and realizing the movie we'd picked was still on the title menu. "But you can pick something else." He scooted over to make room for us on the couch—my only real piece of furniture.

Courtney looked through the DVDs I had. "*Mall Cop*?" she said, holding up one she'd found on my shelf.

"That's probably there by mistake," I said.

She turned to me. "You have the sequel," she said, pointing it out on my shelf. "It's awful, but I like it," she said, handing me the DVD. "I did security for the mall right out of high school."

"Why'd you leave?" Jorge asked.

"Too much bullshit," Courtney said, sitting down on the couch, leaving the middle cushion for me. "Had to stop a mom stealing clothes for her son at the Gap once," she said. "It was really depressing." She cracked open her beer.

"Now you're after Banksy," Jorge said.

"More of a deterrent than an active pursuit," Courtney said. "Like a neighborhood watch."

I popped in the DVD and joined them on the couch.

"Marathon?" Courtney asked.

I hit play, and every now and then, her leg would brush up against mine, making it hard to concentrate on the movie. The occasional arm bumping we did while lifting our beers became more frequent, and I was starting to think we were both doing it on purpose. Eventually, Jorge got up to piss, and I finally got a moment alone with Courtney.

"I'm glad you joined," I said.

"We'll have to do it again," Courtney said. "Without Jorge next time." She squeezed my hand. Jorge came back and we continued the movie, but halfway through the second one, I could barely keep my eyes open. Maybe it was from the weed, maybe from the beer, or maybe from the fact that I'd been up for over nineteen hours, but I fell asleep on Courtney's shoulder.

WHISTLE WHILE YOU WORK

She didn't wake me before she left, but she left me a note saying she was going to use my key to lock the door, that I would have to find her to get it back.

A FEW WEEKS before I would be getting my walkie-talkie, Shawna came in in a bad mood.

"What's up?" Jorge wanted to know.

"They're threatening to make me part-time," Shawna said. "Saying they can't afford all three of us and a security guard for one building."

"That's some bullshit," Jorge said.

"Isn't it technically two buildings?" I asked.

"It doesn't matter," Shawna said. "Look, y'all know y'all are like family, but they think the security guard is why there hasn't been another break-in. I have to let one of you go," Shawna said. "I'm sorry, but I can't be on hourly with no benefits."

"I've been here longer," Jorge said.

"There's gotta be something we can do," I said.

"I tried everything," Shawna said.

"What if we get Courtney fired?" Jorge said.

"What?" I asked. Courtney and I had been seeing each other since that night at my place. I'd even told my parents about her during our phone calls. She worked overnight and I had to be up super early, so it was mostly weekends, but those weekends were the best ones I'd had in a long time, maybe ever.

"Sorry, bro, but that's just how it is," Jorge said.

"How?" Shawna said.

I couldn't believe my ears.

"I'll just quit," I said.

"Don't be stupid," Shawna said. "You got a good thing here. Don't throw it away over someone you've known less time than some of the shits I've had," Shawna said. "How?" she asked Jorge again.

"We paint the wall."

THE NEXT NIGHT, I stayed with Courtney for her overnight shift. Shawna and Jorge had said we had to do it together, that we were a crew. They said they were glad I had someone outside of work but that I needed to get my priorities straight. They said all I had to do was make sure she didn't catch them while they snuck in and painted one of the rooms on the fourth floor, that once the school realized a security guard wasn't solving their problem, they would put in the cameras and we'd never have to deal with it again.

"You should go home and get some sleep," Courtney said. We were doing a round on the third floor. Courtney would stop at each classroom, open the door, and turn on the lights, like an RA at summer camp.

"I'm off tomorrow," I said. I felt too guilty to sleep anyway.

Courtney turned off the lights and locked the door behind us.

"We could check out that craft beer place then," Courtney said.

"It's supposed to be nice out," I said.

We were about to walk into another room when the elevator dinged.

"Did you hear that?" Courtney asked.

I couldn't believe those lazy assholes hadn't taken the stairs.

Courtney jogged over to the elevators and pressed her ear to the door.

WHISTLE WHILE YOU WORK

"It's moving," she said and started pushing on the up and down arrows.

"Should we call somebody?" I said.

"Come on," Courtney said, heading for the stairs. I followed her, trying to lag behind, hoping Jorge and Shawna had enough time to escape, but Courtney didn't seem to care if I caught up or not. I sneezed as loudly as I could in the stairwell, trying to alert Jorge and Shawna.

When I opened the door to the hallway on the fourth floor, Courtney was already in the room that had been vandalized once before. I jogged over and peered in, pressing myself against the wall like I was in an action movie, but all I saw was Courtney crouching down to check under the desks. Maybe Jorge and Shawna had backed out or decided to do a different floor or room, thinking I was going to choose Courtney over them.

"See anything?" I asked.

"No," she said. "Let's check the other rooms."

"Maybe the elevators were just resetting for the night?" I said.

Courtney shook her head, told me she hadn't ever heard the elevators make any noise with no one inside the building. I followed her to each of the rooms on the rest of the fourth floor. When they were cleared, Courtney turned to me and said, "Up or down?" as if to say *Dealer's choice*. We made our way down to the second floor and looked into each of the classrooms.

"I feel like John McClane," I said, but Courtney didn't laugh; she was in full security mode. Courtney was small, but I started to worry she was going to tackle Shawna and hurt Shawna's back or break Jorge's nose if she caught them.

We made our way up to the fifth floor. And right when I thought Jorge and Shawna had made it out safely, Courtney said, "Look," and waved me up the last two steps. She pointed down the hall, and I could see an open door with the light on inside the room.

"Let's get 'em," Courtney said.

"With what?" I asked, checking my pockets, like it would magically make handcuffs appear.

"I got a baton," she said, taking it from her belt. With that, she instructed me to follow her in a crouched position, and we made our way to the door halfway down the hall on the right. When we got there, without any hesitation, Courtney ran in and shouted, "Stop right now!" I stayed outside the door and considered running if I heard Jorge's or Shawna's voice, but after a few seconds of silence, all I heard was Courtney calling me into the room.

Inside, I saw the paint that Jorge had bought and hidden in the janitor's closet earlier that day and two paintbrushes.

"Maybe they're in the bathroom?" I offered, but I knew they weren't coming back. I figured the sound of us running up the stairs or their own shadows probably scared Jorge and Shawna enough to make them back out of the whole thing.

"I don't think so," Courtney said. She kicked at one of the paint cans, then bent down to open it. "Think Shawna carried one, or did she make Jorge carry both?"

"What?"

She stood up. "I saw the paint earlier," she said. "Same brand, same color."

Shit.

"Has it been y'all the whole time?" she asked.

"No," I said. I tried to think of a way out of it, but the look in her eyes told me there was no point in lying to her. I tried to make her see my side, saying I'd stuck up for her but that

Shawna had two grandchildren and not enough in her 401(k) to retire early. I said I'd justified the thing in my head by convincing myself that Courtney had experience and could easily get a job somewhere else.

"I'm sorry," I said, disappointed in myself.

"Would you have told me eventually?" she asked.

"Probably not," I said. It was the truth. Jorge and Shawna, for good or bad, were the closest thing I had to family. Aside from them and Courtney I had no one, but I'd been forced to choose a side.

"That's good," she said, and smirked at me. "Loyal," she said.

"Woof," I said.

"I guess that means you won't tell on me either," she said, bending down to pick up a paintbrush and dipping it in the neon-green paint. "What are you waiting for?" she said, tossing me the other brush.

I caught it, and walked over to her.

"What are you going to do?" I asked.

"We," she said, and instructed me to uncap the other can.

"We could get fired," I said.

"Fuck this job," she said.

With that, she swung the paintbrush like a baseball player, getting paint on the carpet, the ceiling, and the wall. Some of it even splattered the back of her uniform shirt and the picture on her badge.

"Come on," she said, gathering paint in her hands.

I dropped the paintbrush and dipped my hands into the paint and joined her, splattering paint across the desks, on the lectern. On the windows and desk chairs. We splattered paint on the floor and along the tiles on the ceiling in long, flowing streams. We didn't stop until we were out of breath and laughing like schoolchildren, the whole room dripping as though it were melting.

"Let's get out of here," she said. And with paint in our hair and between our fingers, she grabbed my hand and led me down the hall, down the stairs, and into the night, where we glowed under the stars and streetlamps. Easy-peasy.

SAINT DISMAS

Carlito held one end of the rope, Omar the other. The three of us wearing orange vests to look official. Our lookout, Sebastián, hid behind some bushes.

¡Here comes one! Sebastián shouted.

I picked up my shovel and dug out some of the dirt we'd dumped in one of the potholes in the road while Omar held up a gloved hand, signaling for the car to slow down and stop. Things had gotten more difficult for us recently, with the news warning drivers about false checkpoints where men dressed in military or police uniforms stopped vehicles under the pretense of government-sanctioned searches, forced all the passengers out of the car, and then drove off to have the car scrapped or sold. There was talk of rapes and beatings when the passengers failed to comply, and sometimes those things happened even if all demands were met. But we weren't like that. Wouldn't have known what to do with a car if we'd managed to steal one. We just wanted the drivers to empty their wallets, then they could be on their way.

We wanted drivers who were willing to spend money to get dirt off their car but not smart enough to keep us from looking inside. A car with fully tinted windows meant someone who might have more money on them, but we risked more not being able to see the gun or machete they might have inside. Non-tinted windows meant less money, but also that we'd be alive to spend it. The best was a clean car with fishbowl windows—someone with money but too stupid to hide it.

The car Sebastián had just flagged was a silver Toyota with a cracked mirror. The car was dirty and had tints. That was the worst combination: a driver who was not only broke but also potentially dangerous. We'd warned Sebastián about this before, but he was still a kid, barely thirteen. He'd be shaking with nerves and excitement, holding the tip of his dick through his pants to keep from pissing himself, and the moment he saw a car, he'd call out to us, not bothering to notice what shape it was in.

When the car came into full view over the hill, we all got into position. I stood in the middle of the road, leaning against the shovel and wiping my forehead. Omar and Carlito held up the rope with the little orange flags hanging from it. When the car stopped, I approached and motioned for the driver to roll down his tinted window. He was barely visible through the darkness of the glass, but I could make out his sunglasses, his raised hand asking what the issue was without speaking.

I pointed at the road, the potholes, my shovel. Construction, I said.

The man shook his head, then tried to pull forward, but I stepped in front of the car.

You can't go through until we're done, I said.

The man honked his horn. He motioned for us to move, and when we didn't, he honked again. Then again, each honk seeming longer and louder than the one before.

I looked over at Omar, who nodded and let the rope slacken to the ground. We didn't want to draw any unwanted attention from anyone. We'd made that mistake once and almost gone to jail because we kept trying to get the driver to roll down his window while he leaned on his horn. There'd been a police car not half a kilometer down the road and we'd had to take off running into the jungle, leaving behind our rope and vests so we couldn't be spotted. We hadn't tried stopping cars there since. But that didn't bother us much, since we regularly moved up or down the highway when we felt a location was getting too hot. This spot was different, because we'd been there for over a week. The main draws were the uphill advantage on one side, and the two-kilometer visibility on the other.

With the rope dropped, the man behind the wheel let up on the clutch and sped down the road without another look in our direction. We watched his taillights as they got farther and farther away.

¡Sebastián! Omar yelled up at him. You stupid son of a—

¡Here comes another one! Sebastián yelled back.

Carlito rolled his eyes.

¿Does this one look nice? I called out.

I think it's a Mercedes, Sebastián said.

Omar, Carlito, and I exchanged glances. Yeah, Sebastián was an idiot, but we had hammered home what fancy cars looked like, using the auto magazines we'd stolen from the supermarket back in the capital as guides. He'd once let two cars get by us while we hid in the brush, thinking them not worth our while. At least he was good about alerting us to the cops.

We got into our positions and waited for the car's logo to crest the hill. Sure enough, a black Mercedes. I wiped my forehead again, sweaty from anticipation. Omar held up his hand and kept the rope taut with the other. I was already picturing what we would do with the money—ice cream, dinner at a restaurant, a hotel room in the town nearby. We were all in desperate need of a shower and a night when we weren't eaten alive by mosquitos or whatever other creatures crawled around the jungle floor in the dark.

We heard the purr of the engine and watched as the car got closer, but by the time we realized the car was speeding up, not slowing down, it was too late for Carlito and Omar to let go of the rope, and almost too late for me to jump out of the way.

¡Fuck! Omar yelled as the rope burned through his palm and got caught in the wheels of the car. ¡Motherfucker! he yelled, holding his hand and watching the rope get dragged off by the Mercedes.

I stood up and looked in the direction of the car just as the rope got loose and tumbled from underneath the tires. ¿You okay? I asked Carlito. He was standing on the other side of the road holding his left hand. He nodded and looked over at Sebastián, who was running down from his hiding spot.

Holy shit, holy shit, Sebastián said.

When he reached us, Omar smacked him in the back of the head with his good hand. I've told you about saying those words, he said. Go get me some water.

Sebastián looked defiant for a moment, then he laid eyes on Omar's hand. He ran into the brush for one of the gallon jugs of water we had next to the tents we'd made out of tarps and branches. Carlito crossed the two lanes of the highway and sat down next to where Omar and I were standing.

¿How much money do you think he had in his wallet? Carlito said.

Let's not think about that, Omar said. It'll only make it hurt worse.

Sebastián ran back with a jug and gave it to Omar, who uncapped it with his teeth and dumped some of the water on his and Carlito's hands, then took a swig out of it.

¿Does it hurt? Sebastián asked.

It doesn't feel *good*, Omar said. He slid out of his vest and took off his shirt, then wrapped it around his hand. He instructed Carlito to do the same, tucking the end of a sleeve into the folds to keep it in place.

¿Now what? I asked.

Omar looked at me like I had spoken in tongues. We still got about four hours of sunlight, he said, as though blood wasn't soaking into his shirt as he spoke.

I couldn't believe it. You and Carlito can't hold the rope, I said.

Omar was all anger then. I got two hands, ¿don't I? he said.

I could tell that letting that Mercedes get away was going to bother him unless we managed to make enough for a hotel room that night.

Omar took another sip of the water, then held it out to the rest of us. We all shook our heads. Omar shrugged his shoulders and held the jug back up to his lips, letting some of the water run down his chin and onto his neck, down to his flat stomach. He was mostly skin and bones, just like the rest of us, but he had more definition in his muscles. While Sebastián and Carlito mostly got tired, me and Omar gained muscle from chopping wood or walking from town to town when we couldn't get a bus or van to pick us up. Omar was twenty, born three years before me, and just over four years older than Carlito. Sebastián had been a surprise.

All right, Omar said. He capped the jug of water and shoved it into Sebastián's chest. Go get us some clean shirts, he said. One for Jaramillo, too.

I looked down at my shirt. There was dirt all down the front of it and a tear near the navel, where I must have landed on a rock jumping out of the way of the Mercedes.

Sebastián sloshed back into the jungle and then came running out with three shirts. I pulled mine on and tossed the dirty one on the road as a car drove by, heading down the hill.

We're already losing money, Omar said, signaling us to get into position. He leaned forward and grabbed his end of the rope with his good hand, then stared off into the jungle, waiting for us, like a statue, a saint. The patron saint of highway robbers.

THE REST OF the day was more successful. We managed to stop a few cars, avoiding the vans and buses. Too many people meant we could be overpowered and held down until the cops showed up. We'd toyed with the idea of fake guns for a while, but unsheathing our machetes was usually enough to get drivers to comply. Plus, the driver could have a gun, and though most people are hesitant to use them, if we pulled a fake gun on them, they might pull a real one on us.

I think we have enough, Carlito said, counting out the money for a room.

Not if we want to eat, Omar said. He motioned for Carlito to get back to his side of the road.

¡A blue Kia! Sebastián called down from his hiding spot.

Omar nodded. Last one, he said, then waited for us to get into position before lifting the rope.

When the car appeared over the hill, Omar held up his hand, and I made my way over to the driver's side. I motioned for him to roll down his window. He did so without any hesitation.

¿Yes? he said.

Omar and Carlito unsheathed their machetes while I reached in to unlock and open the door.

All we want is your wallet, I said, then saw movement in the back seat. Someone who had been lying down sat up with a jerk. I jumped back, expecting a setup. But then I heard my name.

¿Jaramillo? The voice was familiar, but I didn't know why until the back door swung open and out stepped Leslie. ¿What are you doing? she asked.

Leslie used to live in the same village as us. She was the same age as me, worked at her father's business, same as me, before *Los Ojo Locos* took over the village. They'd come without warning, without plans of negotiating, with violence. Anyone who opposed their plans was never heard from again. The *mareros* were all business, all gold teeth and tattoos—the last thing our parents ever saw. The same thing had happened to Leslie's mom.

I looked at the driver. Mr. Cortez, Leslie's dad.

We . . . , I started. We were checking if you needed directions.

Leslie looked at the unsheathed machetes in Carlito's and Omar's hands.

Sebastián came puffing down the hill in a cloud of dust. Check the trunk, he said.

Ah, Leslie said, nodding.

We just wanted something to eat, I said.

She looked at Mr. Cortez, still behind the wheel. We have some snacks, she said.

We can get our own, I said.

¿What kind of snacks? Sebastián said.

¿Are y'all heading to Peacheque? Carlito asked, ignoring Sebastián.

Leslie nodded. ¿Do you guys want a ride?

I looked over at Omar. No, I said. We still had to stop at least one more car.

The town's near the lake, ¿right? ¿Why don't we meet there later? Leslie said.

Nah, we're good, Omar said.

Leslie nodded. Okay, she said. I'll be there either way. Come find me if you want. With that, she gave me a sad smile and got back in her car. We watched the taillights until the car disappeared around the curb two kilometers away. It was getting dark, and the mosquitos were out. That was the worst part about the highlands. That and the humidity that wouldn't let me sleep. I missed the lowlands on days like that, when you stepped out of the shower and immediately began sweating again. I missed the desert, the wind—unobstructed by leaves— that hit your face. I missed home.

Omar kicked some rocks onto the highway.

There'll be another car soon, Carlito said.

Yeah, then we gotta come back out here tomorrow and do the same thing all over again, Omar said. He picked up some rocks and launched them into the jungle.

It's hard for everyone right now, I said, reminding Omar that it had been difficult since before we'd been forced from our homes.

Seems like Leslie's doing fine, Omar said. Probably holding a rum drink with ice in it right now.

I looked at the ground. It's not her fault, I said.

Yeah, Omar said. If only our dad had also been a coward.

None of us knew what to say after that. It wasn't fair to think that way, but sometimes I couldn't help but do the same. When the *mareros* came in, they offered each family one hundred *quetzales*—enough for a shared meal at Pollo Campero—to leave immediately. To grab their belongings and never come back. Those who stayed, who called the police, who wrote to the government, like our parents had, didn't last the week. Leslie's father was among the traitors who gave up without a fight; he took the money, packed up his things and his daughter, and fled. His wife stayed behind because she refused to give up her home.

When the *mareros* came for our parents, me, Carlito, Omar, and Sebastián snuck out the window in our room; we heard the gunfire in the kitchen but didn't stop running until the sun began to shine on the highway. We'd been running ever since, just like everyone else who'd made it out alive. All of us, cowards.

Omar picked up one last handful of rocks and threw them as hard as he could. We heard them as they echoed down the cliffside, hitting branches and trunks and other rocks. He wiped his hands on his shorts and grabbed one end of the rope, holding it with his good hand; the one wrapped in his bloodstained shirt, limp by his side. The rest of us looked at each other but didn't say anything. Got into place just as some headlights made their way around the curb.

IN THE HOTEL room in town that night, I couldn't stop thinking about Leslie.

I'm gonna take a walk, I said.

Omar let Sebastián escape the chokehold he had him in. ¿Since when?

I'll be back soon.

Omar put his hand on the door as I tried to open it. We don't need her help, he said. I pushed past him and heard the door slam shut behind me.

The night was warm, same as always, and the streets were crowded. Vendors sold tacos and ice cream out of carts, souvenirs from small booths, though why anyone would want to remember this place was beyond me. Younger kids chased one another and dodged oncoming traffic. Drivers honked or yelled at them from their window. Down one of the three streets that made up the town, the *elotero* could be heard ringing his bell and shouting into the night.

The lake was calm, disrupted only by the sound of fish jumping in and out of the water. I bent down and picked up a small stone illuminated by a streetlamp and skipped it across the surface of the lake. I was reaching for another when I heard Leslie say my name again, as if she was still surprised to see me.

I was hoping you'd come, she said. She hugged me, and I couldn't remember the last time I'd been held in someone's arms. I'm sorry, she said. It's just nice to see another person from home.

I know what you mean, I said.

¿Should we walk?

I nodded. The water lapped at the shore, and the wind carried the sounds of the vendors and children in town as though they were messages in a bottle.

¿How long has it been? Leslie asked.

Almost two years, I said. It was something I tried not to think about. Each day felt like the one before it as we struggled to survive.

¿Is this what y'all've been doing? Leslie asked.

Basically.

I couldn't tell what Leslie was thinking, but I knew she wasn't judging me. I was sure that she and her father had struggled at first, too, and that no one had been willing to help them either. The government ignored us. The cops ignored us. Said we should have been prepared. And for the longest time, I couldn't understand why *Los Ojos Locos* wanted our town. But Omar finally figured it out while looking at a map, plotting where we would set up our next trap. It's right between these two big cities, he'd said. They're using it as a hub.

¿What about you? I asked Leslie.

She sighed. It wasn't any easier, she said. She looked up at the full moon. We moved around a lot, just like you.

I knew what she meant. We were like turtles, carrying our houses on our backs, settling wherever we could. Leslie put her hands in her pockets and told me she and her father had tried to go to the capital, but the *maras* had also taken over their family's neighborhood there. She told me they'd finally found a place outside Quetzaltenango, but her father couldn't get a job and ended up selling cold drinks by the side of the highway. At least until his foot got run over while he was handing someone a drink through a car window.

We've been looking for a place to work where we don't have to walk too much, she said. She looked over at me to check if I was listening, as if I could somehow ignore what she was saying. I think we might stay here a few days, she said.

There are worse places.

We walked quietly for a few moments. ¿How long have y'all been here? she asked.

A week, I said.

¿And you stop cars every day?

I nodded.

¿How do you not get caught?

I shrugged. We don't make much.

Leslie nodded thoughtfully. ¿Can I help?

I couldn't tell if she was joking. I don't think Omar would let you.

She was quiet for a few seconds. Tell him I know a way to make you more money, she said.

¿How?

She stopped walking and smiled at me. Trust me, she said, he's going to be begging for my help.

NO FUCKING WAY, Omar said. We were by the side of the highway again, the sun just beginning to rise, when he noticed Leslie walking up the road. I hadn't told him the night before because I knew he would say no, but if she showed up while we were already here, he would have to at least listen.

It's a good idea, I said.

We barely make enough without having to split it with someone else. He looked toward Leslie, who was close enough to hear us now. We don't need anybody else, he said.

Good morning to you, too, Leslie said.

Get her out of here, Omar said to me.

¿Jaramillo told you my plan? Leslie asked.

¿To give you all our money? Yeah, he told me.

Think about how many more cars would stop, I said.

I only want a fifth, same as you, Leslie said.

¡Carlito! Omar shouted. Grab the rope.

Carlito looked both ways, then crossed the two lanes to the other side of the highway, scared to upset Omar any further.

I scooted closer to Omar, away from Leslie, and whispered to him. Just one car.

Omar was holding his end of the rope. He looked at me out of the corner of his eye and let out a long exhale. Fine, he said.

I smiled at him and patted him on the back. I turned to Leslie, who was already pulling a small knife from her purse. She made a few rips in her ankle-length skirt, then grabbed two fistfuls of dirt and covered her shirt, her arms, and her hair with it. She spread out her arms like, *¿What do you think?* Omar rolled his eyes, but I gave her two thumbs up.

With that, Leslie inched toward the road and lay down. Omar shrugged his shoulders, mumbled under his breath, and stood by her head. Carlito crossed back over to us and followed Omar's lead. I kneeled down by Leslie's feet as Sebastián ran up to his hiding spot.

A few minutes later, we heard a car engine.

A Ford, Sebastián shouted down to us.

We held our positions, trying our best to look worried. As the car summited the hill, I waved my hands to flag it down, while Carlito and Omar pretended to check Leslie's pulse. They cradled her head, checked her breathing. When the driver noticed Leslie's body, the car began to slow down and the driver rolled down his window.

We need some help, I said, sounding panicked.

¿What happened? the driver asked. He pulled over and put his car in park.

She was crossing the road, I said. She must have got hit.

The man unbuckled his seat belt and opened his door. He walked over to Leslie, Omar, and Carlito. As soon as he reached them, Leslie sat up with her little knife and told him to empty his wallet.

¿What is this? The man put his hands in the air, and Omar made quick work of his pockets. He shoved the man's cash into his hoodie while Carlito ran over to help me search the car. We found some snacks, some unopened water bottles, and some clean clothes to hawk or grow into. There was also a new tire we could sell to the mechanic in town.

We unloaded everything, then told the man to leave.

Not a word about this, Omar said—the same thing he said every time. How seriously drivers took him, I could never tell. Or we'll find you and take more than just your shit.

The man walked indignantly to his car, stopping to take one last look at us before slamming the door shut. He shifted the car into gear. He left so fast, the tires kicked up dust and sprayed us with pebbles as he sped off down the road.

The very first car, I said when the driver was finally out of sight.

It was probably luck, Omar said, counting the money in his hands.

I could tell he was happy about it, even if he was pretending not to be. When he caught us watching him, he hid his smirk, pocketed the bills, then told us all to get back to our places. ¿You think we made enough to retire or something?

Leslie and I exchanged smiles. Then she lay back down on the hot road.

HOLY SHIT, HOLY shit, Sebastián said, and this time, Omar didn't smack him in the back of the head. By the end of that first day, after we'd sold the tire and the expensive cameras and phones we'd found in a car full of tourists, we'd made more than we had in the last couple of months combined.

Don't get too happy, Omar said. She's leaving soon. He counted out some bills and gave Leslie her share as we stood outside the hotel. The sun was setting to the sound of beer bottles opening.

This is more than my dad would make at work, she said, fanning out the bills and bringing them to her nose. Maybe I can convince him to stay longer.

No need, Omar said. We're moving, too. Spot's too hot now anyway. He walked inside, and I followed.

We should do it again tomorrow, I said. We could use her help while she's still here.

Just because it worked once doesn't mean it'll work again, he said. Besides, he said, turning to talk to Leslie, ¿what would your dad think about what you're doing here?

Leslie shrugged. Not sure he'd care, she said, folding the money into her pocket.

Omar snorted. One day doesn't make you a highway robber, he said. Stop trying to act like one. He led the way to our room, and I signaled for Leslie to follow.

One more day, I said. We can't make this kind of money on our own.

¿Why not? Omar said. We can get Sebastián to play dead and it's the same thing.

¿You really think cars would stop for a bunch of guys standing on the side of the highway? Leslie said.

¡Enough! Omar yelled. He threw the empty pizza box from the night before against the wall. We had a good day, let's not fuck it up by talking stupid. He sat down on the bed and began taking off his shoes.

I was scared to say anything else. Omar's temper had always been bad, but it had gotten worse since we'd left home.

The only good thing about it was that no one had ever picked on me at school. Not after Omar knocked a kid's head through the wall in the cafeteria when he tried to take my lunch. I hadn't asked for his help, and I was afraid to thank him for it.

¿What if I moved with y'all? Leslie said.

Omar and I turned to look at her.

We could hit a few spots, and after I made enough to last me and my dad a few months, I would leave.

Omar shook his head. You don't know anything about this life, he said, taking off his socks and tossing them on the floor. He was silent for a minute, and we waited, hoping he would change his mind. Now get the fuck out of my room, he said. And with that, he leaned back in bed and covered his eyes with a pillow.

I followed Leslie out. I'm sorry, I said, carefully closing the door behind us.

¿Why's he being such an asshole? Leslie asked. She was walking down the open-air corridor, like she was trying to get away from something.

He's just scared, I said. Now that we were outside, I got a good look at her hair, at all the dirt she'd have to wash out after helping us.

I guess this is goodbye, then, she said and extended her hand.

I'll talk to him, I said, not shaking, hoping she'd give me another hug.

It's whatever, she said. If he doesn't want to make money, that's on him. Maybe I'll see you down the road, she said, patting her pocket with the cash in it. Then she spun back around and left me there, longing after her.

When I got back to our room, Omar was waiting for me in the doorway. ¿Why'd you tell her no? I said, pushing past him.

We're better off without her, he said, following me into the room.

¿Are we? I noticed that he'd picked up the empty pizza box. He'd just been pretending.

Look, she's cute, I get it, but we can't be taking on another person.

She can look out for herself, I said.

Yeah, but I have to look out for all of you, Omar said. She's not family, she's not my responsibility, and I don't trust her.

We all lost things back there, I said. That makes her family.

Omar let out a long sigh. ¿Why don't we get something to eat? We can talk about it over a *chela*.

I'm not hungry, I said.

Yeah, you are. Come on, I'm buying.

I FOLLOWED OMAR to a seafood restaurant. On the way there, Omar bought a small bottle of rum and put it in his back pocket. He almost never drank, mostly because we didn't have the extra money to spend on alcohol, but also because we had to be up early every morning to start collecting. At the restaurant, he ordered a Coke and a glass and kept adding more and more of the rum. By the time Sebastián and Carlito found us, Omar was pretty drunk.

¿What's up, guys? Omar said.

Carlito looked at me like, *¿What the fuck?*

¿Why are you so happy? Sebastián said.

Sit down, Omar said. He kicked two chairs out for them.

A waiter came by. ¿Can I get you anything to drink?

Water, Carlito said.

¡No! Get what you want, Omar said.

The waiter looked at Carlito and Sebastián. Just water, Carlito said. He sat down. I heard we're leaving tomorrow.

¿That bitch tell you that? Omar said.

Stop talking about her like that, I said, pushing Omar in the chest.

Yeah, she did, Carlito said.

He just wants to fuck her, Omar said.

I stood up and balled my fists, ready to take a swing. Last time we'd gotten into a fight was when we argued over whether or not we could steal a twin mattress tied to the top of someone's car. I think that even then, I knew we couldn't drag that thing around, but I was tired of sleeping on the ground, tired of waking up with a branch or rock digging into my spine. Omar had given me a black eye and a busted lip then and we didn't talk for days. It had been the rainy season, and we took turns sleeping outside because we couldn't stand being under the same tarp together.

Fuck this, I said, swiping a biscuit from the table. I put it in my mouth and held it between my teeth, then flipped Omar off with both hands.

As I headed for the exit, I could hear him calling after me, but I didn't stop to listen. I walked outside and passed beggars and people on their way home from work. I went past people sharpening their machetes and people sweeping their front stoops or playing dominoes. I walked past children kicking around soccer balls and setting off small, handheld fireworks. I walked past the vendors selling fruit and ice cream, and finally made it to the hotel, where the front-desk worker nodded and waved me through.

When I got to the room, I realized I didn't have the key. Maybe that's what Omar had been saying when I left. I turned the knob anyway, and the door creaked open. I guess we'd forgotten to lock it. Inside, everything looked exactly as we'd left it, except for the fact that Leslie was standing in the middle of the room holding something in her hands. When she saw it was me, she let out a sigh and wiped her forehead with the back of her arm.

I thought it was Omar, she said, as if that explained what she was doing in our room.

I stepped inside and felt like I was the one in the wrong place.

¿What's that? I nodded at her hand.

She shoved the bills in her pocket, then looked me right in the eye. You'll make this back in no time, she said. She took a step toward me, but I blocked the door. I left you some, she said, extending a hand; not at me but at the door handle. She took another step, the tips of our shoes almost touching. You understand, ¿right? Her lips were right below my ear. I'm sorry, she said, then twisted the doorknob. The bottom of the door hit the back of my heels, and I stood there for a second before moving out of her way.

LATER THAT NIGHT, Omar pulled all our belongings out of the drawers and threw them onto the floor. He tossed around our clothes and the few toys from when Sebastián was younger. He snatched and pulled the tarp we used as a tent with such force that our machetes and gallon jugs of water fell from the dresser to the floor. We watched as he unfolded the tarp and shook it out, looking on either side of it, like he was doing a magic trick.

¿Where is it? he said, digging back into the drawers as though he'd missed something.

The next morning, we walked down the road, sticking out our thumbs hoping someone would give us a ride, but no one stopped. The only person who pulled over was a bus driver, but we didn't have the fare. We dragged our feet and kicked the trash lining the highway gutters. When the sun began to set, we entered the jungle and hung our tarp. Looking up at it was almost like looking at the night sky, except there were no stars.

We never made as much money in one day as we had that day with Leslie. Even when we did get Sebastián to play dead, no cars stopped, and we went back to using the rope. Sometimes Omar would be asking for a wallet, and all I could do was look in the back seat, hoping to see Leslie sleeping or waiting to make her move—to take us for all we had. What do you call someone who robs the robbers?

A thief, Omar would say again and again. And next time I see her, I'm cutting off her hands. He'd wave his machete in the air and bring it down on the hooves of a dead animal by the side of the road, like he was practicing. I don't think she did it out of spite or anger but out of necessity. I think she was desperate, just like us, just like that thief they crucified with Jesus. He stole because he had to, our mother had said. And God forgave him. I thought about that a lot: how Jesus said the thief would dine with him in heaven that night. Sometimes I picture it—Omar, Sebastián, Carlito, and me, maybe even Leslie, all up there sitting at the right hand of God. Sometimes I can almost taste the wine.

HEART SLEEVES

———————————————

It started with stick and pokes. A smiley face here, a curse word there, even an ex-girlfriend's name on the side of my neck. Teyo was the same way, collecting them like stamps or quarters. So by the time the tattoo gun came into play, we'd been practicing on each other's bodies for years.

Shit looks dope, Teyo said, wiping my arm with Vaseline.

I looked down at my forearm. The colors bled into each other and the lines looked shaky, but it did kind of look like a multicolored jaguar head, if you squinted real hard.

Hell yeah, I said and flexed my muscles. The jaguar with the droopy eye and uneven teeth moved in disagreement.

Who's next? Teyo said. He looked around the living room. We were all smoking joints and sipping beers, but I knew no amount of weed or alcohol was going to convince Sol or his friend Manuel to step up to the plate. They looked at each other with bleary eyes and waited for the other to say something.

Fucking losers, Teyo said.

Next time, Manuel said.

My moms would flip, Sol said. He was twenty-two, a few years younger than me and Teyo, and splitting the two-bedroom apartment with us.

Whatever. I gotta go see Nadia anyway, Teyo said, grabbing his fake leather jacket off the back of his chair. He checked his reflection in the storm door, readjusted his Pittsburgh Pirates snapback, and pulled up his black cargo shorts. Catch you assholes later, he said and slammed the door behind him.

Nadia was Teyo's girlfriend of nine months. They'd met at work, where they tossed dough and sprinkled cheese on motherfuckers' pizzas for eight bucks an hour. Plus tips, the manager always said. But let's be real, there were never any tips; at least not for the tattooed fuckups sweating their balls off next to the brick ovens in the back. Anyway, Teyo had started bringing her around the apartment, and I'd wake up in the middle of the night to take a piss in the shared bathroom and find her in the kitchen with her short shorts, her nipple rings reflecting the refrigerator light bulb. It didn't take long before I was in love, the tattoo of the barn owl on her chest always staring back at me when we fucked.

Think he'll get her name tattooed around his asshole? Sol said, making Manuel spit out the beer in his mouth from laughter.

Goddamn it, I just mopped, I said. It was a lie. Place hadn't been cleaned since before we moved in, and there were half-empty bottles and cans of cheap beer all over the place and cigarette ash in the carpet. Clean that shit up, I said.

Manuel got up to find a napkin or paper towel to soak up the beer. Sol looked over at me. It was just a little beer, he said, but we both knew it wasn't about that.

TEYO CAME HOME that night like I'd never seen him before—happy.

Bruh, you will not believe this, he said, extending a sheet of paper at me. I hadn't moved all day except to shit and make a sandwich with the butt ends of a month-old loaf of bread, and I felt glued to the couch. I took the flyer from him and squinted at it.

Nadia thinks me or you could win it, Teyo said.

The letters finally came into focus and I realized—through the haze of weed smoke choking my brain—that I was holding a flyer for a tattoo convention, and at the bottom of the flyer, in flaming letters, was an announcement about a competition. 27th Street Tattoo and Piercing was looking for an apprentice and would have a booth set up at the convention for people to stop by and show off their portfolio for a chance to enter.

It's only twenty-five dollars to get in, Teyo said.

Even if it was free, I said, we've only had the gun for like, what, twenty-four hours? You've literally only done one tattoo with it.

Oh, shit. Let me get a pic of the one I did earlier. Teyo pulled out his phone and snapped a picture of my arm. First one, he said.

How're you gonna get a portfolio by—I looked at the date on the flyer. What's today?

It's in two weeks, Teyo said. Flyers have been up for, like, a month already. He lit a cigarette. I always hated when he puffed cigs inside, 'cause smoke would linger and float into my room, get all over my shit—clothes, pillowcases, everything.

How the fuck you gonna put something together by then? I asked.

I don't know, man. You got skin, I got skin. He took a long drag on his cigarette. We could practice on each other.

It was the last thing I wanted.

Don't people practice on pigs and shit? I said.

Yeah, but where're we gonna find a cop that's not gonna arrest or shoot us?

We laughed at that.

What's so funny? Sol said, coming into the living room.

Bro, you been sleepin' on my bed again? Teyo said.

Nah, man, just usin' your computer, Sol said, wiping the sleep from his eyes.

Teyo wants to do this, I said, handing Sol the flyer.

Oh, sick!

That's what I said. You gonna let me practice on you or what?

I don't know, man. Fernando's jaguar looks kinda . . . , Sol said, trailing off.

Badass?

Wonky.

Fuck you, Teyo said. Don't nobody wanna tattoo your pimply-ass skin anyway. Teyo flicked his cigarette at Sol's chest, where it exploded.

Fuck, Sol said, slapping at his shirt.

Am I the only one who cleans around here?! I said.

Who you trying to impress? Teyo said. He sat down on the couch and looked at me. I didn't say nothin'. I think Nadia's coming over later, Teyo said, lighting up another cigarette.

Sol looked at me knowingly. What is it about that girl? he said. She's kinda fugly.

You just mad she wouldn't fuck you with your own dick, Teyo said.

Oh, yeah? What about Fernando? Would she fuck him?

Nah, Teyo said. He puffed on his cigarette. She wouldn't do that to me.

Everything got quiet after that, just the sound of the box fan in the corner and the low hum of the fridge.

I'm gonna get another beer, I said, getting up off my chair.

Get me one, too, Teyo said.

I stopped to take a piss in the bathroom, and by the time I got back to the living room, Nadia was sitting on the couch with Teyo.

Hey, Fernando.

Sup? I said, giving her a nod and tossing Teyo his beer.

Teyo tell you about the contest? she asked. She was in a sleeveless shirt and cutoff shorts, her legs all nice and tan from sitting by our building's pool, the one with green water that they never cleaned. She had her hair down. It was darker than mine, almost black, and way longer, had tattoos on her hip bones, upper arms, and calves.

Yeah, I said. Teyo put his arm around her, the tattoo of some horror movie villain touching her bare shoulders. I think we're gonna win, I said.

Nadia smiled at me, just barely, then looked away.

Yeah, you need a job, Teyo said.

I'd been fired the week before for flipping out on a customer. She said I hadn't given her her change and that she'd seen me pocket it. She made a scene about it until Max, the manager, came over and asked what was going on.

This *employee*, the woman had said, is stealing from you.

Truth is, Max had been looking for an excuse to fire me ever since he caught me toking up in the walk-in. And he did so on the spot when I refused to empty out my pockets and started calling them both assholes. I hadn't taken that woman's change, but that wasn't the point. Back in Guatemala, where my parents are, people had also treated me like that. My eyes were always wandering, and people thought I looked shifty. I would walk into a *comedor*, and even though the food was in the back where I couldn't steal it, the owners would watch me until I left. Same thing happened when I'd go down to the lake in Amatitlán—people would be out swimming, but they kept their eyes on their shoes and wallets or sunglasses as long as I was on the shore. I still haven't stole nothing, I just look like I might, I guess.

Too bad I'll be the one getting the apprenticeship, Teyo said. But you can have my job after I quit. He laughed and grabbed Nadia by the hand, leading her to his room. I'm sure Max will be desperate enough to take you back, he said, then shut the door and locked it behind them.

Teyo was always doing shit like that then—saying he'd toss me his sloppy seconds. It hadn't been like that before, back in school when the only reason anyone would date him was because he knew me. I was the one who wanted to be a tattoo artist, I was the one who did my own first stick and poke, Teyo just copied me hoping to get laid. And it was never really about that for me, although it did help that American women saw me as dangerous or different. They would approach me the way they would approach a rabid dog—with caution, but with plans for curing it. I never liked that, but what teenager was going to turn down sex? And once Teyo found out that my first stick and poke had gotten me a three-way, he was all about it, showing off his jacked-up, home-done Playboy bunny outline.

That's why I liked Nadia. She never looked at me like I was an outsider or thought of me as exotic, the way people prob-

ably thought about her, too. She looked past all that, straight
down into who I really was—an artist with dreams of opening
his own shop, if I ever got out of my own way, as Nadia would
say. We'd lay in the back of my car, off the exit near the pizza
place, back near the park, where the trees would hide the car,
and fuck. We'd almost got caught by Teyo once, when he came
home from work on his lunch break. Nadia'd had to sneak out
of my window, like we were teenagers, and we'd taken to using
my car more often than not.

On one of those afternoons we'd spent fucking and smoking, she'd asked me what I wanted out of life, and I'd told her
I didn't know. But she knew. I'd talked enough about it while
stoned in the living room with her and Teyo. If I got stoned
before we had sex, I would always end up asking her to run away
with me.

Where? she said the last time I'd asked, calling my bluff.

Anywhere, I said.

That's how you end up nowhere, or somewhere you never
wanted to be, she said.

And she was right. That's how I'd ended up in places I
never asked to be: the States, where my parents had sent me
to live with my aunt when I was five—and I only returned to
Guatemala during the summers they had enough money for
a plane ticket—hoping I would have a better life here. That
apartment, working dead-end jobs with a dream that was
never going to come true, while listening to Teyo fuck the
woman I loved or thought I loved. And I was a good artist.
I had sketchbooks, though I rarely drew anymore, opting for
weed and heartbreak instead. But maybe that was just who I
was—someone with unfulfilled potential, which looks a lot
like standing still.

THE NEXT DAY, Teyo was banging on the door to my room at six a.m., like we were in boot camp. I opened the door, crust still covering my eyes, breath like dog shit.

Let me knock one out before work, he said.

What?

I can do one of your old sketches. Teyo's eyes were open wider than I'd ever seen them, like he'd been doing blow instead of smoking cigarettes. I knew the gun would end up being a bad idea somehow, but I never thought it would be from too much ambition. We'd found the thing—a Hatchback Irons spider—on sale at a tattoo supply outlet and split the cost, plus the cost of a box of Eternal tattoo ink and needles.

The gun's too loud, I said. Motherfuckers are tryin' to sleep. I was mostly worried about myself, but I was sure the people on the other side of my bedroom wall and below our feet wouldn't be too pleased about waking up to what sounded like bees shoved into a microphone.

It's not that loud, Teyo said.

Ask Nadia, then.

She had too much to drink last night, Teyo said. She's been throwing up for the last hour. Let me see what you got. Teyo shoved past me and turned on the light. He stepped over my pile of dirty clothes and used the remote next to my bed to turn on the five-disc stereo system. He turned it down low and messed with the levels, waiting for me to relent. Maybe I felt bad about the whole thing with Nadia, and that's why I let him share my body with me, or maybe it was something else, but whatever the case, I went to the bathroom to splash water on my face and got out my sketch pad. I tossed it at Teyo, who was now sitting on my bed, setting up the machine. He stopped and flipped through my drawings, occasionally holding the pad up to me when he saw one he liked. Finally, he found one I'd drawn for me and Nadia but had never shown her. It was a tribal drawing of the Maya god of the sun, Kinich Ahau, and the Aztec goddess of the moon and fertility, Coyolxauhqui.

Looks dope, Teyo said.

Yeah, I said, then brought in a chair from the living room, where Sol was still passed out on the couch, next to the wall where Nadia was probably still dreaming. I sat down and pulled up the fabric of my basketball shorts to reveal my right thigh.

Teyo stepped on the pedal a few times to test the voltage. Ready? he said.

I nodded, then leaned my head back and closed my eyes, pretended I was lying down next to Nadia.

I SPENT THE rest of my day driving through town looking for HELP WANTED signs. If I didn't find something soon, I wouldn't even have the twenty-five dollars to get into the convention. I checked with chain restaurants to work as a server, looked for bartending jobs at independently owned spots that wouldn't require me to get a certificate, and was almost desperate enough to stop by a couple of fast-food joints, but I couldn't bring myself to imagine what I'd look like in that kind of uniform, with the little visor and everything.

Finally, I stopped by a few tattoo shops to ask if they were looking for artists. Most said no, but even the ones that said they were asked me for a portfolio, which I didn't have. I'd already done this a few times before, so I'm not sure what I thought had changed—maybe I was hoping it was my luck that had. How could someone gain experience and resources to get good at something without having the money to spend to do it?

Like an ouroboros, my ex had said, lifting up her hair to reveal a tattoo of a snake eating its own tail on the back of her neck. And goddamn her if she wasn't right.

I decided to stop by the 27th Street Tattoo shop. Outside, the windows were covered with flyers advertising the upcoming convention, and nothing but motorcycles and expensive cars sat in the designated employee parking spots.

What's good, homie? the receptionist said. He was bald with a tattoo on the top of his head extending down the sides of his face and a 4XL T-shirt.

Sup? I said. I was seeing if y'all were hiring.

We got that competition at the convention coming up. That's about it.

I pulled my sketch pad out from my baggy jean shorts. I'd almost left it at home but convinced myself to bring it at the last moment; had to do the same thing in the car. Before I could say anything else, he held up his hand, a tattoo of an eye on his palm, and told me they weren't looking at anything until the convention. I nodded, folded the sketch pad in half, and put it back in my pocket.

Shit, dog, he said suddenly, you're bleeding. He pointed at my leg. Sure enough, blood was running down my thigh, down my shin, and into my sock.

Shit, I said. I'd been so nervous, I thought I was just sweating extra hard. The receptionist handed me some paper towels from behind his desk just as one of the tattoo artists came up from around the back.

What's goin' on? he asked.

Got some new ink this morning, I said. We didn't have anything other than some plastic wrap, so that's what I'd used to cover up my tattoo.

Let me take a look, the tattoo artist said.

I lifted the right side of my shorts, and you couldn't even make out the tattoo from all the red liquid pooling under the wrap.

Damn, son, the tattoo artist said. You're lucky my next appointment isn't until two, he said, then waved me over to the back, to his station. Sit down, he said, pointing at his wrapped-up tattoo chair. He put on his gloves and turned on one of the floor lamps, which he pointed at my leg. He removed the wrap, then soaked paper towels in something he squirted from a clear bottle. He wiped away the trails of blood that had dried all the way down to my ankles. When we could finally see the tattoo, he opened some Aquaphor and began to rub it on my thigh. He let out a whistle as he looked at it more closely.

Got some scarring going, he said. Where'd you get this done?

A shop outside of town, I said.

Some shaky lines, barely any solid ones. And this shading, he said, shaking his head. They should shut that place down. He finished rubbing the ointment on my skin, then pulled out some large square bandages that looked like the things they put in with meat packaging to soak up the blood. He taped a few to my leg, then slapped my tattoo over the bandaging.

Fresh-tattoo slap, he said.

How much do I owe you? I said over the sting.

It's all good, he said. He snapped off his gloves and thew them in the trash. Heard you had some sketches, he said. I tried to pull them out of my pocket, but he stopped me. Nah, he said. Anyone can draw. You have to practice on real skin, pig skin if you gotta, but something with blood and muscle. You're young, he said, even though he couldn't have been more than twenty-eight. You got time.

But I didn't, or at least it didn't feel like it.

How am I supposed to get a portfolio ready by next weekend? I asked.

That's not what I meant, he said. Plus, he said, all you really need is one good tattoo that shows off your skills, something that'll wow us. Original, bold, clean. He patted me on the back. Now get outta here, he said.

I thanked him for cleaning up my tattoo.

Sure thing, he said. Stop by the booth next weekend.

I told him I would, but I don't think either of us expected me to show up.

THE WEEKEND CAME and I still hadn't done a tattoo, 'cause no one was willing to let me use their skin. I'd asked Teyo, but he'd made up some bullshit excuse about not wanting to be a tattoo artist and a canvas within a week of each other. Sol and Manuel were still being chickenshits, and there was no way I was asking Nadia. I'd even called everyone in my phone saying I would do it for free, but not a single person returned my call.

Come on, Teyo was saying. We were sitting in the living room with Sol. You don't want to help out a friend?

It's not that, Sol said. It's just, I don't know what I would get. Or where.

Fernando's got sketchbooks full of ideas, Teyo said.

Nah, man. Let's just keep smoking. Maybe order some pizza or something. I'll pay for it and everything.

Teyo groaned, then got off the couch and went into the kitchen.

I'm sorry, Sol said.

It's cool, I said. Probably wouldn't've won anyway.

We sat on the couch and watched a commercial for Zoloft and then one for a rehab facility. We were on a commercial about tattoo laser removal when Teyo came back into the living room with three Solo cups.

My bad, y'all, he said. The pressure was getting to me. He set the cups down on the coffee table and shook himself like a wet dog. How about some drinks? He handed us each a cup. To my new future job, he said, then took a long drink. Sol and I looked at each other and sipped what tasted to be rum and Cokes, heavy on the rum. I thought y'all were happy for me? Teyo said, crossing his arms over his chest.

You're right, I said. You're gonna kill it. I raised my cup a little and drank half of what was in the cup. Sol followed suit.

All right! Teyo said. Why don't we get this party started? I'll text Nadia and see if she can come through and bring some of her friends with her. I think they're supposed to be goin' to some club, but maybe they'll stop by, if you know what I mean.

Teyo was happier than usual, and I couldn't blame him, I guess. He thought he was about to make my dreams his own. The only thing that really scared me was how much better the money would be for him if he got the job. It wasn't likely, not with his tattooing, but crazier things had happened. And if he was making enough, he wouldn't have to live here anymore, and then I'd never get to see Nadia. I tipped the rest of the drink into my mouth. It was a lot, and as I stood up to get more, I felt it all sloshing around in my gut.

Take it easy, Teyo said, or you're gonna pass out before Sol. He laughed.

Fuck you. I can hold my liquor, Sol said.

Prove it, Teyo said.

Sol tipped back his cup, and streams ran down his chin and onto his shirt. When he finished the drink, he threw the empty cup across the room.

All right, all right, chill, Teyo said. Gonna end up with rum dick before the girls get here.

We sat down and passed around a joint, and pretty soon, I wasn't too worried about the convention anymore.

I guess it just isn't my time, I said.

Teyo smacked me in the back of the head with an open palm. *Cállate* with all the mopey shit, he said. Then he nodded over at Sol. I got you an early Christmas present, *pendejo*. He got up off the floor and snapped his fingers in front of Sol's face. He slapped him a few times for good measure, then smiled.

Looks like you got a canvas, Teyo said.

I looked at Sol. What the fuck you talkin' about? I said.

Don't play stupid, Teyo said. I got you exactly what you wanted.

A lawsuit?

Sol can't afford no lawyer, Teyo said. He ran into his room and came back out with the equipment, all sealed in two little silver travel cases. Set him up, Teyo said.

He's gonna wake up, I said.

Nah, I gave him a little help.

I looked at Teyo.

My moms has trouble sleeping, so the doc gives her some pills. He shrugged his shoulders. People sleep through tornadoes on this shit. He was plugging in the equipment and setting the paints on the table.

I'm not tattooing him without him knowing, I said.

Teyo stopped what he was doing and turned to look at me. You tellin' me this is the first time you've done something behind someone's back? he said, then began tying the bands around the gun. You need a canvas or what? 'Cause I could use more practice if you're not gonna do it.

Okay, I said. I couldn't tell if Teyo knew about Nadia, or if I just felt guilty. I took the drink out of Sol's hand and then leaned him back on the couch. Teyo handed me a disposable razor.

Do it on his forearm, Teyo said.

That's too visible, I said. I'm going to use his thigh.

I ain't helping you pull down his pants, Teyo said.

I unbuttoned Sol's shorts, angled him one way and slid the shorts down on the opposite side, then angled him the other way and did the same thing with the other side, careful to keep his boxers on, until the shorts were down to his ankles. I shaved his thigh of all the black hair and used a Sharpie to freehand something on his skin, something I thought he would think was badass—a phoenix rising from the geographical outline of Mexico. Then I looked at Sol's face and silently asked him to forgive me. I told him I would make it up to him, hire him as a receptionist once I opened my own place, then I dipped the needles in black ink and brought them down on his skin.

THE DAY OF the convention, it was only me, Teyo, and Nadia. Sol had disappeared, along with his meager belongings. He'd woken up the day after I tattooed him, screaming, cursing, and almost knocking down my door, saying his mom was going to kill him and that he, in turn, was going to kill me. It wasn't until Nadia came out of Teyo's room and talked him down that he finally packed up his things and left. Teyo had come out of his room to tell Sol to shut the fuck up, then gone back to bed, so Nadia came into my room after Sol slammed the door shut behind him.

You shouldn't have done that, she said, running her hands through my hair.

I wanted to show you I was trying, I said.

She shook her head. We can't treat bodies like that, she said. They're not disposable.

We let Teyo use ours all the time, I said.

No, she said. Only you do.

At the convention, with a picture of the tattoo I'd done on Sol burning a hole in my pocket, I followed Nadia, thinking about what she'd said and looking around. There wasn't a single person not covered in ink. We looked like newbies in comparison. There were people walking around in nothing but thongs, showing off every square inch of flesh covered in art. I saw tattoos of snakes, hot dogs, a Jif peanut butter jar, people's pets. My earrings had nothing on some of the people's plugs you could stick your fist through. The air smelled of green soap and sweat, and over the sound of all the conversations was the constant buzz of the tattoo guns.

We'd gotten a map of the convention layout at the front and were zigzagging our way to the 27th Street Tattoo booth. We were running late because my car wouldn't start and we'd spent over an hour trying to get someone to help us jump it. In the end, Nadia had to borrow her brother's car and drive down to pick our asses up.

Hurry up, Teyo was calling back to us, almost at a jog.

When we got to the booth, there were people gathered all around, same as at every other booth, but there was something a little extra there. People were holding their breath, watching the tattoo artists look through portfolios.

We're here, Teyo said, trying to push his way to the front of the crowd. Nadia and I followed close behind.

Artists are already making their decisions, the man behind the rope said, the spider tattoo on his bald head moving as he clenched his jaw.

Come on, man, Teyo said. We're better than all those ass-holes.

People rolled their eyes and groaned and shouted at him to shut the fuck up, while me and Nadia stood behind him looking at the ground. Finally, the tattoo artist from 27th Street who'd cleaned up Teyo's work came over to where we were standing. He started to ask what was going on but stopped when he saw me.

I see you made it, he said.

Teyo turned to look at me like I'd betrayed him, like I hadn't already betrayed him.

You got a piece? the tattoo artist asked me.

I took the folded, laminated picture out of my pocket and handed it to him. My friend has one, too, I said, nodding at Teyo.

All right, the tattoo artist said, taking my picture and Teyo's photo album, I'll toss them in there. He went back to where the artists were deciding on the top five pieces. We waited for what seemed like a lifetime, and every time my picture or Teyo's album got passed from one artist to the other, Nadia would squeeze our shoulders or pull on our shirtsleeves, equally ex-cited for both of us, I thought.

The tattoo artist came back and handed a piece of paper to spider-head, who began to read. If I call your name, please come forward.

The first three names went by in a blur. Then the fourth name was called, and it wasn't mine or Teyo's. The man called

the name again—Nichole Ferris, he said—but no one came
forward.

Skip it, the tattoo artist said, and spider-head went on.

James Soderbarker, he said, moving down the list to fill the
fourth spot. James whooped from the back and made his way
behind the rope, throwing up both middle fingers on his way
to his booth.

And lastly, the man said, Fernando Escudo.

Oh, shit! Oh, shit! Nadia said, wrapping her arms around
my neck.

Spider-head unhooked the rope to let me through.

I turned to Teyo and put my hand out for a handshake, but
his face was frozen in anger.

Think you can take whatever you want, Teyo said, then gave
me a shove that pushed me behind the rope. Security looked
over, but I held up my hands and said it was cool, that that was
how we congratulated each other. Security backed off, but they
kept their eyes on Teyo.

Congratulations, the tattoo artist said to me as I sat down
at the last station left.

It was luck, I said. It's only 'cause Nichole didn't show.

Sometimes that's all it takes, he said.

Spider-head stood in the center of the roped-off section and
spoke loudly enough for all of us, including the crowd—all cheers
and hushed speculations about the outcome of the competition—to
hear. We were going to get two hours to tattoo an open canvas.
There was no style requirement. The only requirement was that it
be good, the man said. Then he asked the canvases to join us. We
watched as they walked in, men and women of different ages and
skin tones. I counted them as they came in, wondering which one
was to be mine. But I counted only four.

The man called for the last canvas by name, but no one stepped forward. He turned to the tattoo artist.

The tattoo artist nodded and walked back to my station. And sometimes your luck runs out, he said. You can't compete without a canvas.

I looked over at Teyo. He was angry, but he owed me. What if I got someone to volunteer?

The tattoo artist shrugged. That's fine, he said, but we can't wait for you. He nodded at the man in the center to continue.

The man clicked the stopwatch around his neck and told us time was ticking.

I ran over to where Nadia and Teyo were still standing.

I'm not fucking doing it, Teyo said.

I let you tattoo me everywhere, I said.

And I let you fuck my girlfriend.

People were watching us now.

You don't let him do shit, Nadia said. I choose what to do with my body.

Then choose me, I said.

Fuck you, Teyo said, grabbing Nadia by the hand. Come on, he said. But Nadia snatched her hand back and turned to face me. Only the rope stood between us, and I reached to let her through, but Nadia put her hand on top of mine, stopping me. She leaned in and gave me a kiss on the cheek, then grabbed Teyo's hand and led him through the crowd.

I once asked Nadia what it would take to get her to break up with him and run away with me. Money? I asked. No, she'd said. A heart transplant. I didn't get it then, how she could prefer him, but it makes sense now: you can't help who you love. The last thing I saw before they blended in with the rest of the crowd was Teyo's tattooed finger flipping me off as they walked away.

I guess that's it, I said.

The tattoo artist shrugged. You *could* tattoo yourself, he said.

Really?

No rules against it, he said.

I looked at the tattooing station, then at my arm, the opposite side from where Teyo had tattooed the fucked-up jaguar. In my mind, I cleaned the area, shaved it, and prepared the needle—a 12 gauge—then dipped it in the ink.

Fifteen minutes gone, the tattoo artist announced.

In my mind, I brought the needle down to my skin.

The tattoo artist walked back to where I was still standing, unmoving. You gonna start? he asked.

That was the question, wasn't it?

CAÍDAS

La Cascada de Agua Caliente is situated between El Estor, Guatemala, and not much else. It borders El Lago de Izabal on one side, El Boquerón on the other. The only way there is by boat or on wheels, down the two-lane—occasionally one-lane—highway. This is where Don Sergio Mendez lives, where he works, has worked for all but the first two years of his sixty-nine-year-old life. His father—long dead, God rest his soul—looked after the waterfall, a job that has since fallen to Sergio. It isn't an official position acknowledged by any local government, meaning there's no income to report, no taxes to pay, not even a donation exemption—not that Sergio makes enough to be giving any money away—but it also means not being able to contact the local authorities when they're needed.

Recently there's been this American tourist, constantly leaving empty water bottles and candy wrappers strewn about the dirt parking lot. Sergio has asked him to please clean up after himself, but the boy hasn't listened. He seems young— early twenties, that age at which he thinks he's invincible, untouchable. Sergio remembers that age well, but he doesn't remember ever behaving like an animal.

"The pigs," Don Sergio said to the boy the last time he spoke to him, asking him to pick up his discarded cereal box, "even they don't make such a mess." Don Sergio pointed to the wild animals, four piglets and six adult pigs that roamed near the winding stream and knew to stand farther back during the rainy season, the way they were doing then. The boy kicked the cereal box in the direction of the animals, then got in his car and drove off.

Now Sergio watches him get out of his car and into the back seat, from which he will reemerge in his tiger-print swim shorts. Don Sergio's main job, other than cleaning up the trash left behind by tourists, is guiding them into unmarked parking spaces. For this service, he asks for one *quetzal*. Once a car is parked, he tells the driver that he will watch it for an extra four *quetzales*, which they can pay him once they're done swimming. In the last two months alone, he's stopped someone he didn't recognize from stealing a car radio and a group of teens from popping the tires of an SUV. No one has ever turned down his offer—especially tourists, who, Sergio has heard from the tour bus drivers, can afford the seventy-five American cents he's asking for in exchange for protection. No one except the boy who litters, who makes eye contact with Sergio as he drops his food wrappers on the ground.

The boy emerges, towel across his shoulders, and the children, the ones who are there every day swimming and begging for spare change, run to his side. All of them with palms cupped and extended, saying they have sick relatives or that they haven't eaten in days. But, as usual, the boy ignores them. Most other tourists will give at least one *quetzal* to the group, sometimes one *quetzal* per child, or some of the chips or cookies they have in their cars to eat during their travels. But not him. Not even a glance at the little kids surrounding him, tugging on his shirt, leaving wet mud stains on the sleeves.

The boy pushes his way past them, but they don't give up. They call after him asking if he has extra food or clean water, saying they'll watch his car. But Sergio knows they won't. The moment he's out of sight, they'll forget all about it, walk back down to the bank until they hear the crunching of gravel under the tires of the next vehicle. The boy makes it to Teressa, the woman who stands at the edge of the path through the jungle that leads to the waterfall. She sells coconuts and coconut water for five *quetzales* each, chopping the coconuts herself in front of her customers—no fresher than that. But again, the boy walks by, not even acknowledging her presence.

Sergio spits on the ground, makes his way from the rock where he spends most of his time to the boy's car. It's a small, silver thing with tinted windows and Central American license plates—rented, from the capital probably. Sergio prides himself on respecting people's privacy. Not once has he looked inside the windows of a tourist's car to check if it's a manual, to see what kind of food they have in the back seat. But this time, he can't help himself. It's the fifth day in a row this boy has shown up, and Sergio, if nothing else, wants to know how many more pieces of garbage the boy plans to throw away here.

Sergio looks around, then, taking his cowboy hat off and pocketing the orange in his palm, he cups his fingers around his eyes and tries to peer through the tinted windows. It's no use—they're too dark. He walks to the front of the car and leans over the windshield and tries to look inside again. He can make out what he thinks is the steering wheel, maybe even a cup of coffee in the cup holder. He's wiping the windshield free of dirt with his shirtsleeve when he sees the boy's face reflected in the black tint. Sergio jumps back in surprise. He didn't hear footsteps on the gravel or the sound of the children begging for change.

"What the fuck?" the boy says.

Sergio doesn't know these words, but they don't sound good; they sound accusatory.

Sergio steps back from the windshield, recomposes himself, and says, "Even though you are not paying me"—he waves a finger back and forth in the air—"I was looking after your car." Sergio notices the dirt on the front of his shirt reflected in the car's windows and wipes it away, places his hat back on his head.

"Spying is what you were doing," the boy says.

The group of kids has heard the commotion and is running over to the car to see what's going on. They're all babies—the youngest is probably two years old, the same age Sergio had been when he'd first started coming to work with his father, and the oldest is Roxanne, twelve years old, overweight even though she hardly eats. They respect Sergio because of the stories people tell about him—how he saved a boy from drowning, how he fought off a tiger when it tried to take one of the children—but none of those are true. Especially the one about the drowning boy.

"I've been watching your car since the first day," Sergio says. "Nothing bad will happen to it." Sergio makes the sign of the cross over the car as if blessing it.

"Liar," the boy says, this time in Spanish. This boy with shaggy hair. With whom is he here, or is he traveling alone? Why did he take an instant disliking to Sergio? Without another word, the boy reaches into the back of the car and pulls out a bottle of sunscreen. Then he reaches in and pulls out a grocery sack. Sergio thinks he may finally be giving the kids something to eat, but instead, the boy turns the sack upside down and out fall empty Coke bottles, multicolored food wrappers, and a half-eaten burrito. The boy kicks the trash. Napkins Sergio will have to track down flutter in the wind and blow across the parking lot, under cars, and into the trees. The boy then throws the bag in the air, slams the car door shut, and presses a button that makes the car beep, before turning around and walking back toward the waterfall.

The kids follow, begging for money again. Some chase the napkins, tearing to pieces the ones they manage to catch. Sergio calls out for them to stop, but they can't hear him over their laughter. Tired at only midday, back already aching, knees swollen, Sergio sighs, pulls the orange out of his pocket and peels it before beginning the work of cleaning up the trash.

WHEN THE SUN has almost set, Sergio grabs his walking stick and makes his way up the path to the waterfall to check for stragglers, the littering boy long gone. He finds a group of teenagers sharing a cigarette, emptied beer cans laying on the rocks nearest them. Sergio recognizes them; they're local boys. He calls them by name, letting them know he'll tell their parents what he's caught them doing if they don't pack their things and leave. Slowly, the boys climb out, wet swim trunks leaking water down their legs. They grab their towels, throw on their shirts, and snatch up the battery-operated radio they brought with them. They climb the stairs leading to where Sergio stands, each of them muttering a goodbye or thank-you as they walk by him. Sergio doesn't climb the steps unless he has to, but he knows he's climbed them more times than anyone else.

The boys disappear down the trail, their voices echoing in the jungle, and Sergio follows slowly behind, until he reaches the path he and his father made by walking to and from the waterfall every day. He turns up and begins the ascent, each step harder than the last. It's gotten to where he has to stop two or three times during the half-kilometer walk to his house to catch his breath. When he finally makes it, he leans his walking stick against the door, lights his oil lamp, and sets it on the kitchen counter. On the gas stove, he heats some tortillas, then dips them into a plateful of refried black beans. He's running low, but it's Wednesday, and Doña Linda's son, Roberto, will be by on Friday with his groceries for the week.

Sergio finishes his food, washes his plate using a clean bowl to scoop clean water out of the basin filled with that week's rain, and dries his hands. He takes out the money he made that day and adds it to the peanut butter jar scrubbed clean that an American tourist once gave him. With what he's made so far, he'll have enough for the groceries and not much more. He twists the lid back on the jar and places it in the cupboard behind a box of cornflakes.

He sits in his rocking chair and reaches for one of the volumes of poetry his father owned. Sergio never understood poetry until after his father passed away ten years ago, two years after his mother, at the age of eighty-five. Ever since then, he's been reading and rereading the collections and trying to write, just as his father had. He reads a few poems from an anthology and then pulls out his notepad and pencil. There, in faint handwriting made even harder to read in the dim lighting, is a poem Sergio has been working on for weeks. He reads over the lines he's written, scratches out a word, tries to replace it with something else, then writes the same word again.

He sets his pencil down, then rubs his eyes with his fingers. He gets up and carries the lamp to the other side of the room, where his bed sits. He places the lamp by his feet, and it illuminates the empty bed his father used to sleep in. He considers getting up to brush his remaining teeth—crooked, yellow, chipped—but doesn't have the strength. He takes off his shoes and socks, blows out the lamp, and lays his head on the pillow.

He's asleep before he knows it, dreaming of things he doesn't wish to remember: the boy whom some say he saved—his brother—drowning next to one of the caves under the waterfall, the way his brother—seven, two years older than he—had said, "I bet I can hold my breath for two minutes," and how Sergio had said he didn't believe him. How his brother had taken in a gulp of air, playing it up as if filling an extra pair of lungs in his chest, then closed his eyes and swam under the falls. How Sergio had stood by the edge of where the hot water from the falls meets the cool water of the lake below, holding his breath as if he were the one underwater. After several minutes, Sergio began to worry. He'd already had to take in three more breaths of air since his brother disappeared under the current.

His father had been walking up the trail then and called down to him from the top of the stairs, asking why he was standing there staring at the water like he'd never seen it before.

"Jonathan has been holding his breath forever," Sergio said.

His father laughed. "Don't believe everything he tells you," he said and went on to explain that there were two small caves under the rocks behind the waterfall filled with pockets of air. He said kids went in there all the time, but to still act surprised when Jonathan resurfaced. Sergio smiled, covered his mouth with his hands to keep from laughing, and waited for his brother to reappear.

"Your mom said lunch is ready," his father said. "Come home when Jonathan's back."

Sergio nodded, then turned his attention to the water. Time passed, and his father eventually returned and saw him standing in the same spot looking at the waterfall. In the dream, Sergio can see his father running into the water calling Jonathan's name. He sees his father going under the water and staying under for an impossibly long time before coming back up with Jonathan in his arms. He sees his father crying, calling for help, and then pounding on his son's chest, shouting for him to wake up, Jonathan's face already pale from being underwater for so long, his fingers like the tips of leather moccasins.

"The man who loses /," his father had said one night, years later, finishing his first poem, reading it aloud to Sergio, "a child /," he said, pausing briefly to let out a sound of pain—a cross between a sneeze and a wheezing. "Will drown himself / in sorrow in this life / and will burn for his mistakes in the one after."

THE NEXT DAY when the sun begins to peek over the horizon, Sergio walks down to the waterfall. No one else is there yet, just a few pigs downstream with their snouts in the water. Sergio unbuttons his yellow short-sleeved shirt and khaki pants. He lays his cowboy hat next to his towel and wades in, shivers as the coolness touches his shins, thighs, groin. But soon, he is standing under the warmth of the falls, heated by a natural spring somewhere up in the mountains. He lets the water run over his face and back as he scrubs himself with a bar of soap, steam rising off his body and the surface of the lake. The sun is halfway over the horizon now. That's when Sergio sees it.

He wipes the water from his face. There, in the aboveground cave behind the waterfall, are what appear to be empty beer cans. He wonders if it was the kids from yesterday. But when he steps behind the waterfall to get a closer look, he realizes he's wrong—they're spray-paint cans. Sergio grabs one and shakes it. It's light, empty. Sergio looks around the cave. Gone are the days when he could climb on top of the rocks in there, bathe in the steam that rises and fills the inside like a sauna. He does his best to look as far inside as he can, but there's no sign of the paint. He steps back through the waterfall holding the two empty cans, and there, in letters almost two meters tall, he sees the words *Espía esto, cabrón* next to a drawing of a large uncircumcised penis spraying cum on the surrounding rocks.

Sergio's intake of breath is so sharp, he begins to cough and stumbles, and accidentally drops the cans into the water as he tries to regain his balance. By the time he's recovered, he sees that the cans are no longer by his side but around the bend of the stream. Sergio dresses quickly and uses his walking stick to climb the eighteen steps to the top as fast as his knees will let him. He shuffles through the empty dirt parking lot, past the pigs bathing in the river, up the narrow, one-lane pathway, cleared of trees to make way for cars and buses. He heaves past the kids who are setting up their lemonade stand at the entrance to the falls. He sees their father napping under the tree by the road, where he will charge tourists fifteen *quetzales* for entrance into the park. Out of breath, feeling like he's underwater from the humidity, Sergio walks down the side of the main road that leads to El Estor, but in the opposite direction.

By the time he reaches Doña Linda's house, he feels as though his lungs are sloshing around inside him. He knocks on her door and is greeted by a half-asleep woman—Linda's daughter, Sadie.

"Your mom," Sergio wheezes.

Sadie helps him inside. He doesn't want to know how he looks, but he knows it must be bad if Sadie is taking pity on him. She's in her mid-twenties now, but when she was eight or nine, she had come home from a friend's house early and found Sergio and Linda, naked from the waist down, eating empanadas at the kitchen table. She never forgot or forgave him. Even though she'd never met her father, Linda told Sergio that Sadie always thought her father would come back for her, wherever he was.

"I'll get you some water," Sadie says. It's the last thing Sergio wants, but he doesn't say anything, takes the cup when she holds it out to him. "Mom's already at the store," Sadie says.

Sergio nods. He wants to ask Sadie to go get her but doesn't want to push her hospitality. He thanks her for the water, then prepares to walk the other half kilometer down to the little *comedor* Linda owns. But as he stands, he sees the person he's really there to see coming out of the back room.

"Señor Mendez," Roberto, Linda's seventeen-year-old son, says. "I thought today was Thursday." He looks at the floor.

"It is," Sergio says. "I'm not here about the groceries, but I could use your help with something else."

"I'm supposed to help my mom at the *comedor*," Roberto says.

"Yes," Sergio says. He looks over at Sadie, who's crossed her arms over her chest. "She told me it was okay."

"¿I thought you said you were looking for her?" Sadie says.

"We talked about it yesterday," Sergio says. They're wasting time, and if he and Roberto don't get down to the falls before the tourists start arriving, everyone will be talking about how

Sergio can't keep anything safe, how he let a kid deface the most beautiful part of the town. "Go ask her," Sergio says. He'll explain everything to Linda later, but right now, he and Roberto need to remove the writing on the wall.

"Go," Sadie says. "I have other things to worry about." She turns and grabs the mop bucket from under the kitchen counter to make her point.

When they're outside, Sergio tells Roberto to run up ahead, that there are two brushes near the back door of his house that he uses to scrub his floors and the *pila*—admittedly not as often as he used to. He tells Roberto to grab them, the dish soap, the detergent under the sink, and a bucket, and to meet him at the waterfall. Roberto nods and runs down the road, his *chanclas* making a slapping sound against his feet, slowly becoming quieter until Sergio is glad he can't hear it anymore. He follows the boy, trying to go as quickly as he had on the way up, but his legs hurt, and his back feels like he's attached sacks of bricks to it.

By the time he gets down the stairs to the waterfall, it's less than an hour before people will begin arriving; some of the kids are already in the parking lot kicking around a deflated soccer ball. Roberto is standing in front of the wall with the graffiti, mouth and eyes open wide.

"Let's start scrubbing," Sergio says, as if removing vulgarities from the rocks is something they do on a weekly basis.

"¿Why would someone do this?" Roberto asks.

"God only knows," Sergio says, handing the bucket to Roberto. "Fill this with hot water."

Roberto rolls up his pant legs and walks along the edge of the water. When he reaches the side of the waterfall, he grabs part of the slick rock formation and holds out the bucket until it's full. He waddles back carefully, trying not to slip or spill. Sergio has already scrubbed the brushes clean in the cool water by his feet. He hands one to Roberto, then drops some detergent into the bucket and stirs it around with his brush.

"You do the top part," Sergio says, signaling for Roberto to climb up on the rocks. Roberto does, and Sergio hands him the bucket to set by his feet. They dip the brushes into the soapy water and lather the rocks over and over, pushing hard on the paint. They sweat, and Sergio's shoulders ache. His back threatens to give out, and his arms shake involuntarily, more and more violently each time he lifts his brush from the bucket. Sergio scrubs and scrubs until his arms go numb, scrubs for what feels like years, like he's always been there pushing against the wall, trying to dig his way through the stone, looking for something.

BY THE TIME Sergio and Roberto are done scrubbing, both of them are covered in sweat, their shirts soaked under their armpits and down their backs, the brim of Sergio's cowboy hat darkened and damp. Sergio thanks Roberto and tells him never to mention this to anyone. Roberto agrees, but Sergio wonders what he'll say to his mother or Sadie if they ask. Sergio climbs back up the stairs with his bucket and goes home to change clothes.

When he gets to the parking lot, there are cars already stationed there, and the kids are crowding around a white couple. The kids extend their palms, and the strangers dig into their fanny packs and pockets for loose change. Sergio hears the crunching of gravel under car tires and walks toward it, ready to direct the car into an unmarked spot, but when the car rounds the bend, Sergio recognizes it immediately. With legs like dead stumps, Sergio walks toward the car, as if playing chicken. He steps to the side when he realizes the driver isn't going to slow down and bangs his open palm against the back window. He follows the car until the driver chooses to stop, and begins yelling as soon as the boy opens the door, even though he is still a few meters away.

The other doors swing open, and four more people around the same age as the boy step out from behind the tinted windows. Sergio stops yelling but doesn't stop walking toward the car. When he reaches the group, right behind the kids begging for food and change, the boy turns to his companions, swings a thumb in Sergio's direction, and says, "This is the crazy man I was telling you about."

"We know that guy," one of the girls says.

Sergio ignores her.

"¿Want a beer?" the boy asks Sergio, popping the trunk. He opens a cooler, in which Sergio can see the tops of Gallo bottles buried in what appears to be ten kilos of ice. The boy is trying to act innocent. Sergio knows it. Not once has he offered Sergio anything.

"We'll take it," Roxanne says. Sergio shoos her and the others away, and they run off toward the sound of another car coming down the pothole-filled road.

"You can't drink here," Sergio says.

The boy stares at Sergio, then closes the cooler. He pulls it out of the trunk. "Let's go," he says to his friends, who slam the car doors, towels in hand.

"¿Why are you doing this?" Sergio asks. The trash was one thing, but the graffiti, that was going way too far.

The boy stops, then turns to look at Sergio. He's taller than Sergio, maybe 175 centimeters, white skin, vengeful eyes, and in his American accent says, "Just trying to leave my mark." He spins on his heel and catches up with the others, who've walked by Teressa and her coconuts without a second glance.

THAT NIGHT, AFTER cleaning up all the empty beer cans the boy and his friends left behind, Sergio walks home to find Linda sitting at his hand-hewn kitchen table.

"Roberto told me what happened," Linda says.

Sergio sighs, hangs his hat on the back of a chair.

"I was going to tell you," he says.

"I don't mind that you took him away from work—God knows that boy spends half the time staring into space—but I want to know what you did to aggravate someone to that point."

"So do I," Sergio says, shaking his head, walking to the sink, and dipping a cup into the clean water in the basin. He dips another one and sets it in front of Linda.

"He looks up to you," Linda says, pushing the cup aside. She's lit the oil lamp, and it illuminates the side of her face, the wrinkles there so deep, they look as if they have been carved into her cheeks. She didn't always look like this. When they were kids, years after his brother drowned, they played together, but Sergio always felt like a consolation prize. His brother was more handsome, and Linda had always liked him better, maybe because they were the same age.

Sergio sits across from her, and she reaches her hands to his.

"You know I never wanted kids," Sergio says, and Linda moves her hands back to her lap.

"That doesn't make it any less true," Linda says and stands to leave.

"I'm sorry," Sergio says, shifting toward her.

"Fix it," Linda says. "I can't have Roberto out here working for you for free." She smiles lightly at Sergio, showing him
everything is fine between them, but Sergio knows he's hurt
her. After Roberto was born—different father from Sadie's—
Sergio had played the part of parent, changing diapers, taking
Roberto to the falls during his workday, even staying over at
Linda's place, sleeping on the floor. But once he and Linda
started sleeping together, when it started to feel as though he
was responsible for Roberto and not that he was doing Linda
a favor, Sergio had taken his leave, visiting with less frequency
until his visits dwindled to only birthdays and Christmas.

After Linda's gone, Sergio picks up her cup and takes it to
the sink. He washes his, then hers; uses the same sink to brush
his teeth and scrub his face. Then he turns out the light and lies
down in bed but can't fall asleep. He's scared that if he drifts too
far, the boy will come back and spray-paint more of the rocks.
Finally, to set his mind at ease, he puts on his boots and cowboy hat, and grabs his walking stick and flashlight. The night is
warm, humid, and loud with the sound of insects.

When he's close enough to hear the falls, he thinks he also sees
a flash of light—a flashlight or headlights, he's not sure; he didn't
check the parking lot. He walks on, slowly. The sound of rushing
water fills his ears. Then, sure enough, there it is again, like lightning but dimmer, yellow. He continues on to the stairs, flicking his
flashlight to off. He knows the trail by heart, has climbed it more
times than he can count, but even so, it's difficult in the dark. One
wrong move, stepping too close to the right, and he could fall down
the mountainside to the sharp rocks below. He thinks of turning
on his flashlight again but doesn't want to give away his position.

Then it hits him that he doesn't know what he's planning
to do. So what if he catches the boy spray-painting the rocks?

Will he stop simply because he's been caught? Sergio has already underestimated him once and had to work all day for that mistake. Would the boy hurt Sergio? He doesn't seem like that type of person, but then again, he also doesn't seem like the type of person who would spray-paint the side of a mountain. Maybe he is exactly the kind of person who would do both.

Nevertheless, Sergio pushes forward. When he gets to the top of the stairs that lead down to the waterfall, he sees what he had hoped he wouldn't—the boy, flashlight in his mouth, one hand on the slippery ledge, spray can in the other, and the toes of his shoes on a small foothold—standing dangerously high on the cliffside.

"¡Stop that!" Sergio shouts out to him. But the boy doesn't, just keeps writing what looks to be the words *Eat me*. Maybe the boy's too close to the waterfall to hear him.

Sergio steps down to the first landing. He points the flashlight at the boy's back, then turns it on and shouts, "¡I said stop!"

When the light comes on, the boy tries to spin around on the little foothold on which he's standing. And before Sergio knows what's happened, the boy has dropped his flashlight, has dropped the spray paint, and is falling, backward, off the side of the mountain. He lands on the rocks below in the shallow water, his head only briefly visible as it hits a stone the size of a coconut. Then the boy lays still, his head underwater, until the current begins to wash him downstream.

Sergio drops his walking stick, his flashlight, and holds on to the railing that leads to the slippery rocks below. He almost loses his balance when his boots touch the stones made smooth from years of running water. He pauses to see how far the boy has gone but can't make him out. Sergio starts shouting incoherences, and is then shouting "¡*Stop!*" as if the river might obey him. He slips and is momentarily face down in the cold water.

His chest hurts. He stands back up and tries his best to run alongside the river, but the bank begins to disappear, and soon, he's running through the shin-deep water. Finally, when the water reaches his knees, he submerges himself in it, thinking it will be easier to paddle along than to continue to run and fall. Up ahead, where the water reflects the moon, Sergio thinks he can make out the shape of the boy.

"¡I'm coming!" Sergio shouts. He's out of breath, and water leaks into and out of his eyes. "I'm almost there," Sergio pants. But he doesn't know for sure. Maybe it's too late already. The water, if he were to stand, would be waist-high now, and as he paddles, he begins praying to his brother. "Please," he says, gasping for air. He kicks his legs, and there, right in front of him, is the boy—his body caught between two rocks. "I got you," Sergio says, trying to stand but slipping. "Hold on," he says, reaching for the boy. Sergio's arms and legs burn from the exertion of that afternoon. His shoulders threaten to dislocate, and he feels as though his wrists, sore from scrubbing the rocks clean, are splintering. The boy is heavier than he looks, and Sergio is struggling to lift him.

Finally, he decides to lift only the boy's head out of the water. Sergio can't tell if he's breathing. He pinches the boy's nose shut and tries to breathe into his mouth, but he can't catch his own breath. He leans over the boy and pants between his lips. He forces another breath and blows into the boy's mouth. His head is growing lighter and he's feeling dizzy, but he doesn't stop trying. He takes another breath. Just one more, he thinks. One more. Then another, and another, until he can't take another. And as the world goes dark, his chest burning, Sergio thinks that this must have been the exact way his brother felt. This is what it feels like to leave the world drowning.

BUS STOP BABY

Turned out the third bedroom in the house was a garage without heating, without air-conditioning, nothing but earwigs.

Whaddaya think?

Tim was high off the pipe and scratching at his neck like he was trying to get to something. Eyes like the bare light bulbs hanging from the ceiling in the kitchen.

Is that the bed?

Just as advertised, he said. Try it out.

Maybe later.

It was a mattress they'd pulled from behind an apartment building ten blocks away, but I didn't know that then.

Suit yourself, Tim said. Hank'll be home later. I'm sure he'll want to say hello. He took one last look around, then left.

Alone in the room, I noticed planks of wood had been shoved into the far corners to help keep the roof up and the sliding door shut. I could see them bending under the weight. I set down my suitcase, which held nothing but two work shirts, four long-sleeved T-shirts, some jeans, socks, and boxers, all with holes in them.

There was no other furniture in the room, so I sat down on the mattress. It was damp, but it was hard to say with what. I unzipped the suitcase, reached into a hidden pocket, and pulled out the only thing I would have for dinner, sealed in a baggie, and the spoon I would use to eat it. I had a few dirty cotton balls to use as napkins and a lighter to heat up the soup. When I was done, I shook out the pillow and watched the dust and dirt settle on the cement floor, then lay down, heard the squish of liquid leaking out from the mattress into the cracks in the floor. I stared at the one fluorescent light bulb, the same kind they had in high school, as it started to flicker and reminded myself that this was only temporary.

I WALKED TO work the next day. It was a couple of miles farther than from my last place, but the worst part was the windchill. No, the worst part was not having a coat.

You're late.

I just moved yesterday. The walk is longer.

Take the bus, Shannon said.

Can't afford it.

Did you apply for the reduced transit fare?

I told her I had. Showed them my pay stubs and everything.

Let's not worry about that right now, she said. There's dishes piling up everywhere. Go, go, go.

I was, stereotypically, a busboy/dishwasher. Not at a Guatemalan restaurant, not even at a Mexican restaurant, but at some bougie place with overpriced salads, wraps, and sandwiches. Yet the pay was still shit. So much so that most of the servers, though they risked getting fired, would usually eat customers' leftovers on the walk from the table to the dishwashing station at the back, where they would have to throw the rest into the trash can. I never had an appetite then, but I knew that if I did, I'd be doing the same thing.

I was partway through a stack when Nick came up behind me. Sup?

Elbow-deep in murky water, I said.

Cool, cool. Re-up? he asked, leaning up against the basin.

Can't. Got rent.

Aren't you living with your girlfriend? Nick said, hopping up and balancing on the sinks. Get her to pay it.

Nick always called her that, but she wasn't my girlfriend, she was a friend I'd met at my last job. We were in the waiting business then, and after one of our late shifts, she'd invited me over to her house for food and a beer. She was a vegetarian, and I didn't eat, so it was easy to pretend I was, too. Then, a few months later, I stopped going in to work and she texted me. I told her I was going through a breakup and didn't have the bandwidth to show up. She said she understood and that I could text her if I needed her. Turned out I did. She let me move in after my ex kicked me out, and we drank and smoked, but I always slept on the couch. I made it all of five weeks before she found my kit and told me she wasn't ready to see another OD. I told her I only used recreationally, but she didn't believe me, told me to pack my shit and leave.

Got kicked out, I said.

Damn, that sucks. Nick hopped off the sink. If you ever need anything, he said. And for a second I thought he meant it, but then he patted his pocket. Anytime, he said. I got you.

BY THE TIME I got back to the house, Tim and Hank were already there and already getting there. And they weren't alone. Two other guys sat laughing on the couch, beers in hand.

Moises, Hank said, putting his arm around me like we hadn't just met the day before, like we were good, old friends. Want a drink? A hit?

I'd never smoked crack before, wasn't one for uppers, so I told him no.

Gonna kill the vibe, man, Tim said.

Sit down, one of the guys on the couch said, tapping the spot beside him, sending dirt and spilled cocaine into the air.

Hank gave me a shove, and then I was sitting. The man next to me handed me a beer.

How do you know Hank? he asked.

I don't, I said. I know Tim. Kind of.

Tim and I had met in high school. He dropped out sophomore year, and I dropped out the year after. We'd run in the same circles—going to house shows or backyard bonfires—but we'd never been close. Then when I put up a social media status saying I needed a cheap place to live ASAP, he was the only person who responded.

Cool, the man said and put his hand on my thigh.

Oh, I said, thank you, but no.

Fernando's straight, Tim said, rolling his eyes.

Take a hit of this and it won't matter, Hank said, passing me the pipe—glass, burnt on the bottom and still hot.

I'm good, I said. I headed toward the garage.

I saw your setup, the man who was sitting next to me on the couch called out. No heating in there, he said.

I closed the door behind me, would have locked it if I could have. I flipped on the light and watched it sputter to life. On the mattress was an envelope. It was from the mass transit authority. On one side, Kylie, the woman who'd kicked me out and driven me here, had written "I hope this helps." She must have dropped it off. I opened the envelope and inside was my bus pass. I lay down holding it, my shoes still on. In the other room, the music came on loud, and I could hear all four of the guys singing along to pop songs I'd never heard. Pretty soon, the singing stopped and the moaning started. I knew if I was ever going to get some sleep, I would have to fix up, so I did. After, I lay back on the mattress and let it all fade away, that bliss better than any orgasm.

A FEW HOURS later, I woke up to shouting. Not joyous sounds but angry yelling. I rolled over and tried to ignore it, but then there was a loud bang, and then another. I didn't want to walk out there, so I waited for things to die down. When all four of the guys finally seemed to move back into one of the bedrooms, I grabbed my sweater, kit, and bus pass and peeked out the door. Inside, everything was turned over. The dining chairs were on their backs, the lamp and lampshade were separated, and there were two new holes in the wall. I heard more arguing in the bedroom and thought I would make my escape before any of them came back out and saw me.

The night was motionless, like it had been put in deep freeze and nothing was warm enough to move anymore except me. Every footstep I took felt like it would echo for miles. I walked to the main road and then to the first bus stop I could find. I waited, shivering in the wind. When I saw the bus approaching, it moved so smoothly, like it was on train tracks. The doors opened and the inside was an invitation, heating promising to keep me warm, at least until the last stop on the route. I tapped my card to the machine, and it made a sound of approval unlike any I'd ever heard before. The bus was empty and the halogen lights were blue. I walked to the very back and sat down. I could feel the engine vibrating down my spine, and I jerked a little as the bus took off, but pretty soon, I felt like I was floating without having to shoot up. I dozed on and off until we reached the last stop and the bus driver called back for me to deboard.

Once outside, I called up to the driver. Will you be back? I asked him. He shut the doors in my face and was soon nothing but blurred brake lights. I crossed the street to the bus stop on the other side and waited for him, but he never came. Instead, an older woman driver pulled up to the stop and opened the doors. I climbed the stairs, but there was no peace on this bus. It was loud and smelled like too much perfume. Inside, the bus was almost full. Nothing but drunk college students shouting and kissing and rubbing up against each other. I almost climbed back down, but the driver had closed the doors behind me and was waiting for me to scan my bus pass. I wanted to tell her to let me out, but I couldn't feel the tips of my fingers, so I said nothing, scanned my card, and searched for the first open seat.

I walked past students not much younger than me, all of them sporting school logos and Greek letters on their jackets, and took a seat near the back of the bus, next to a man with a long salt-and-pepper beard and a heavy coat, hood pulled up over his head. He scooted farther away from me when I sat down, as though if he tried hard enough, he could climb into the glass that made up the window.

Sorry, I said.

He grunted and looked over at me out of the corner of his eye. I think he saw something in me, something kindred, because his posture relaxed a little.

What day is it? he asked.

Friday? I said.

He nodded. Should have known, he said, then pulled a bottle of cheap whiskey out of his coat pocket. He took a swig and then held the bottle out to me, all behind the seat in front of us. I took it and wiped the back of my mouth with my sleeve. It burned my throat, like someone had struck a match and lit a cigarette in my esophagus.

Thank you, I said.

Not what you're used to, he said, but it'll keep you warm.

I don't know how he knew, and I didn't ask.

Where are you headed? I asked.

He laughed a little. Nowhere, he said. Got nowhere to go, nowhere to be. A pure bus stop baby.

I know what you mean, I said.

Nah, he said, not yet.

We were quiet for a few moments, listened to the chatter of the coeds all around us.

Got any family? he asked.

Disowned, I said.

A place?

A garage.

Better than a bench, he said. He took another swig from the bottle and offered it to me again, but I shook my head. Why are you out if you got a spot?

I told him, and he listened. Almost like he wanted to. And maybe he did. Maybe only those of us with nowhere to go and nowhere to be have time for those who do.

The bus emptied around us one stop at a time, and pretty soon, we were sitting alone in the seats. I learned his name was Al. He was from down south but had a warrant there, so he'd moved north even though the winters were miserable. He had an ex-wife and two daughters, had lost them to his drinking.

He asked me about myself, and I told him about how I was a disappointment to my parents. They'd moved to the States to give me a better future, but with the time they spent worrying about my future, they'd neglected the present, and I'd found something else in the meantime.

What they were worried about most, I said, was me and my brothers growing up on the streets of Guatemala City. They never thought I'd have to grow up on the streets here.

People are quick to give up on you, Al said. And I don't mean you, I mean us.

I nodded.

You got a good head on your shoulders, though, he said. It's not too late.

And in that moment, I wanted to turn my life around, but then he extended the bottle back to me and I took a deep swig from it.

Last stop's coming up, boys, the bus driver called.

Al capped the bottle and stretched in his seat. I scooted out into the aisle and followed him down to the front.

See you next time, Nancy, he said to the driver.

Stay safe, Nancy said and opened the double doors.

Once we were standing outside in the cold, I asked Al why Nancy didn't just let him ride during her whole shift.

They got cameras, Al said. Someone's always watching, but they only care if you mess up. He extended the bottle to me again, but I said no. All right, he said. Gonna head on up this way and find somewhere to sleep.

Okay, I said. Thank you. For the drink.

Take care of yourself, he said, patting me on the shoulder, or bus riding will become your whole life, he said as he shuffled up the street. Before he disappeared around the corner, he waved at me one last time, and I think he really hoped not to see me again.

I crossed the street and waited for the next bus. It didn't take long. And when the door opened, I understood why. It was Nancy, heading back the way we'd come.

Am I allowed to get back on? I asked.

Long as you pay the fare, she said.

I scanned my bus pass and wondered how much money was left on it. At least I had enough to get home. I would worry about getting to work in the morning. I started walking toward the back and could feel Nancy watching me in the rearview.

Come sit up here with me, she said, pointing to one of the seats designated for passengers with disabilities. Reserved for the infirm.

I shuffled back to the front and sat down. The seats smelled like VapoRub and onions. Nancy shut the doors and pulled away from the curb. We glided down the streets, hitting red lights and speed bumps, dodging stray cats and nighthawks. We were halfway to the house when Nancy finally spoke again.

Why are you really out here? she said. I didn't know what she meant. You punishing yourself?

I looked down at my hands. Maybe, I said.

She clicked her tongue and turned down another street. Yeah, she said. Al's the same way. Thinks he doesn't deserve love. She shook her head. Been trying to get him clean for years. Even offered him a place to stay, but he likes surfing those benches.

I got a place, I said.

She nodded. Got a job?

Barely.

We hit a stoplight, and the bus let out an exhale.

Nancy looked at me in the rearview. We're hiring, she said and tapped a sign above her head. The pay was way over minimum wage, and they offered medical and dental. I ran my tongue along my teeth. Couldn't remember the last time I'd brushed them.

I don't even have a license, I said.

Don't matter, Nancy said. Even with a license, you'd have to go through training.

I nodded. Seemed like it was all I could do—nod or nod off. You interested?

I stared at the steering wheel. I don't know, I said.

They're always looking for young folks, she went on. Course, you'd have to drop the habit. Her eyes met mine in the mirror.

Why are you trying to help me? I asked.

She shrugged her shoulders. I see a lot of myself in you. Lost, looking for someone to hear my silence.

We were nearing my stop. Should I pull on the cord? I asked.

Sure. She stopped at the sign, and I stood up to leave, but she didn't open the doors. You ever been to a methadone clinic?

I shook my head but didn't turn around to look at her, just faced the doors, willing them to open.

I could hear her doing something behind me. Here, she said and extended a piece of paper to me. It had her phone number on it. In case you change your mind, she said, then pushed the lever for the doors. I stepped off the bus just as the horizon was beginning to brighten, the colors still dark enough to look like a bruise.

When I approached the house, something immediately looked off. As I got closer, I saw that two of the front windows had been broken and the door was cracked open. I opened the door carefully and looked inside before I stepped in. On the couch were Tim, Hank, and the two guys from earlier, all with eyes like old tomatoes.

What's going on? I asked.

Did you take it? the guy who'd had his hand on my thigh earlier wanted to know.

We can't find the stash, Tim said.

You holding? Hank asked.

I don't smoke, I said.

I can't go to work without taking a hit, Hank said.

We're all in the same boat, Tim said.

Empty your pockets, the guy from earlier said.

Leave him alone, Tim said.

We could call Jesse, Hank said. You got the rent money? he asked me.

I told Tim Monday.

You gotta pay your share around here or you gotta go, Hank said.

He said Monday, Tim said.

I heard what he said, Hank said. Is anyone hearing what *I'm* saying? He cocked his fist like he was ready to punch another hole in the wall.

All I know, the guy from earlier said, is that we need to find it or get some more.

Maybe Jesse'll front us some, Hank said.

I doubt it, Tim said.

My head is killing me, the man who'd been silent up until then said. I fucking hate coming down.

Let's check in here again, Hank said.

They groaned and complained, but they all got up and started turning over cushions and moving around furniture. All of them, all of us, in pain and in need of something to help ease it. Though what had brought on the pain, none of us could really say. A vague sense of unease with the real world, a feeling of loneliness, worthlessness, of not being good enough, of not achieving our dreams, whatever those were that we were too scared to work toward for fear of failing. Past heartbreaks, STIs, or mental illnesses. Could I keep returning to this room, sitting under the same roof?

OPTION A

I'll help, I say. I know I won't get any rest with them banging around in there. They'll probably come into my room anyway, tear the whole place apart looking for their stash. So I get on all fours and start looking around for a baggie that one of them might have already emptied. I turn over things they've already turned over— lamps, the sofa, shoes—and help them rip open the couch cushions and tear down the curtains.

Finally, Hank has a moment of clarity. Shit, he says.

OPTION B

I don't even go back into the garage, with its red-painted walls and sputtering light, my clothes and suitcase. I pull my kit out of my baggy cargo shorts and set it against one of the turned-over pieces of furniture, then walk back outside. No one even notices me leave.

A FEW MONTHS later, Al gets on my bus. He doesn't recognize me at first, but I know him even before I open the doors. When he tries to swipe his pass, I put my hand over the scanner and he looks up, thinking I'm going to deny

I think I put it under one of the floorboards in my room.

We all stare at him in disbelief. Why would you put it under there? Tim asks.

Hank shrugs his shoulders. Didn't want you guys to know where I hid it, he says, laughing a little.

Then they all start laughing, looking at each other knowingly.

Hank runs into his room and after a few moments, he calls out to us. Come help me find it, he says.

We obediently walk into the room, where Hank has already pulled up a few floorboards. I can't remember which one, he says.

Probably one of the loose ones, I offer.

They're all loose.

We all kneel down and begin pulling on boards. There is cursing and sweating as we move Hank's bed and his meager furniture.

Are you sure it's under here? I ask.

him a ride; I can see it in his eyes, the way they aren't completely swimming yet.

Hey, I say. I watch as my face slowly registers for him.

Holy shit, Al says. The bus is full with the afternoon crowd and the passengers all have their own conversations going or their headphones on. What are you doing behind the wheel? he says.

Nancy, I say, then close the doors and pull away from the curb.

She's good like that, he says. You got a new pad now? I nod. Good, he says, then holds on to the bars and makes his way to an available seat. People get on and off, switch seats, and bump into each other. The bus is all but empty save for Al when I get to the end of the route, and I watch as he shuffles back up to the front, staying behind the yellow line.

It was good seeing you, Al says, but I don't open the doors. He turns to look at me.

Yeah, Hank says.

Finally, under one of the last boards in the closet, I find a baggie with little crystals in it. Not even good, clear ones, but ones that will get the job done.

Got it, I say. The searching stops, and I am suddenly the center of attention. I have something they all want.

Oh, thank God, Tim says.

Why didn't you say something sooner? Hank wants to know.

You tease, the man from earlier says. He claps me on the shoulder and takes the bag out of my hands. They all rush into the living room and start loading the pipe.

Want to join? Hank asks.

Yeah, I say and turn a chair back on its legs. I watch as they smoke while I shoot up, blurring the day. All of us have jobs we have to get to in a few hours, but

I would have never met Nancy without you, I say. He waves his hand dismissively. I got a couch, I say.

His eyes focus on mine. And I got benches, he says, then turns to push the doors open. He kicks at them, but I hold them closed. Finally, he leans against the door and starts to cry. You think I haven't tried? he says. I sat in the very same spot you're sitting. And even though it's the middle of summer, he wears a jacket and uses the sleeves to wipe his face. How much longer you think you gonna last up there? he says, pointing at my chair.

Before I can answer, he turns and kicks the door so hard, I think it will break. I open it, scared to get fired, and Al jumps down. He trips, falling hard on the pavement, but he shoots back up before I can put the bus in park. I watch him hobble up the road and think of honking the horn, but he is gone, blending for those few beautiful moments, there are no outside problems or obligations, nowhere we need to go or be, just five junkies fortifying themselves against the day ahead. Counting down the seconds until we can come back again.

into the city, just the way I used to.

I close the doors and put the bus back into gear, then turn around, heading back the way I'd come, but on the opposite side of the road. I never see Al after that, but I remember the night I first met him, how he'd talked about his life and how he didn't get to choose his destiny. He said that no matter what he did, he was destined to become a bus stop baby. And I felt the same—a kind of calling to the bus stop benches. But I hope Al found another way there, the same way I did, and I hope that we only ever see those benches while letting people out at their stops, that we've always got somewhere to be, even if it's only the next stop on the route.

FIGHT SOUNDS

The crew showed up early, early morning. Sun-had-basically-just-set early. Hadn't-even-washed-the-sex-off-my-balls early. They came in like the military used to, all fast and bright and loud, like bullets. I ignored the sound and headlights, didn't see the truck they'd parked right outside my front door 'til I woke up around noon, and by then, they'd already started setting up.

I stepped outside for my first cigarette of the day, and there they were—people with cameras and microphones running around like loose chickens. Some had on headsets. Others sat in seats with job titles on the back: director, producer. People carried lights and set up tents and snack tables. The kids who would normally be running up and down the dirt and gravel road in the center of town stood next to their parents, watching the action from their front steps. I waved at Sarita, whose house was next door to mine, but she ignored me. Had been ignoring me since she found out I was fucking any woman who'd let me, probably heard the one from last night. But, shit, we were young. Early thirties, and I wasn't settling down until my back gave out.

I thought of blowing her a kiss, but I heard Florencio, Sarita's brother, running up the road. He was short of breath from excitement.

"They're shooting a movie," he said.

I lit my cigarette. "No way they got the right place." In Quetzaltepan? What Hollywood people were coming to this shithole to shoot a movie?

"It's true," Florencio said. "They're giving out jobs." He pointed at a line that was forming on one side of the road in the center of town. It led to a few tables with people and paperwork. "Come on," he said. Then he ran back the way he'd come. *Chanclas* slapping against his dirty feet. I still didn't think he'd heard correctly, but if they were going to give a job to Florencio, with his missing teeth and bad breath and lazy eye, then I was going to get me one, too.

I flicked my cigarette against the concrete wall of my house, ran my fingers through my hair, and walked after him. I turned to see if Sarita was coming—I bet she would have looked good on-screen—but she wasn't. She'd leaned into her house and brought out a broom to sweep her front step and my ash and cigarette butt.

We stood in line for over an hour, waiting for our turn and watching all the foreigners shower in sunscreen. As the line moved, word traveled back to us, and we learned that they were shooting what was called a blockbuster. Like *Rocky*. Except this one took place in Guatemala. It was a about a man who ran away from the States after a murder he may or may not have committed. Of course, someone finds him, and there were going to be fight scenes and explosions and fire, and the production crew planned on being in town for weeks. There was so much excitement at the idea of rich *Americanos* spending their money here that I thought we'd be able to power the town just from the electricity in the air.

Everyone in line made small adjustments to their wardrobe as we got closer. People buttoned, unbuttoned, and rebuttoned shirts. Women smoothed out wrinkles in their *huipiles* and straightened their *tocoyals*, while men dusted off their straw hats. When it was my turn, I showed up just like I was. They wanted a real Guatemalan, this is what he looked like—dark skin, scars on my arms, machete at my side, and dirt on my fingers.

"Hello." A woman with brown hair spoke, and a guy who looked like me but with more money, probably from the capital, translated for her.

"Tell her your name," the man said.

"Antonio Banderas," I said.

She smiled at me. She had nice teeth. Like wax from holy *velas.*

The man sitting next to her rolled his eyes. "¿Do you want a job, or no?" the man said.

"Antonio Calebra," I said.

"Like a snake?" she asked.

"No, but close," the man translated.

She filled in my info, then flipped through papers on a clipboard. "Looks like all of the extras with lines are taken," she said. "We have regular extras or foley artists," the man translated.

I had no idea what a foley artist was, but Sarita was big into painting. I figured maybe this would get me back in her good graces, or, at the very least, her bed. "Artist," I said. The woman smiled at me again, then wrote something down on a piece of paper and handed it to me.

"You won't do anything for the first couple of days," the man translated. "Once they have some footage filmed and edited, then you'll meet with Michael. They're building the foley stage right now."

I thanked them, gave the woman my best smile, my I'll-see-you-around smile, and then left. I looked at the piece of paper. All of it was in English, and I didn't understand any of it.

"¿What'd you get?" Florencio asked, running up behind me, holding a similar piece of paper.

"Artist," I said.

"Like, ¿makeup?"

"No, asshole. Like, Picasso."

"Oh," Florencio said. He didn't know who that was. Shit, I hadn't known until Sarita told me. Guess just 'cause they live together doesn't mean they live together. "I got background actor," Florencio said. We were walking up the dirt road that led to our houses, but leaving the town center, I noticed that all six of the main roads that led to the square were full of people holding pieces of paper like ours and smiling.

"¿They give you any lines?" I asked. Florencio shook his head. I bet they thought he was too stupid to memorize anything. Probably was. "That's too bad," I said, then patted him on the shoulder. "We can't all be stars," I said, then went inside my house.

In the kitchen, I ate the last of my stale *pan dulce*, then washed it down with a flat beer from the night before. I thought about work. We were putting a new roof on the church—the only building in town not made of concrete or painted like the houses with their mismatched greens and pinks and yellows, same colors as the tombstones in the cemetery, all of them faded. I wasn't sure how much money the movie people were going to pay me. I should have asked. But even if it was enough for me to quit that shitty job and move out of this shitty town, I'd have to wait almost a week before filming started. That's what the lady at the table had said.

I shook the *quetzales* in my pocket and knew they wouldn't be enough for the bar if I didn't work on the roof today. And the bar would definitely be packed tonight. Not because it was a weekend. It wasn't—it was Tuesday, I think. But because of the excitement. Might even be able to ride that wave into a three-way. Yeah. I traded my sandals for work boots, pulled out another cigarette, then walked to the church, asking God to please let it be Sarita. Sarita and Luisa, the one with the big tits. Please. I flicked my cigarette, could see the cross from where I was. Even Carmela and Brisa would do. Please, Father, bless me.

THE NEXT WEEK, I showed up to the stage they'd built in Señora Nilde's back room. I expected to see paintbrushes, canvases. Even thought they'd give me one of those little French hats. Instead, there were carrots and oranges in baskets. Squash and corn. Some raw beef and cooked chicken. There was gravel and dirt and rocks and leaves. They had pillows and blankets. Brand-new machetes and cowboy hats next to folded sheets and *pastelitos.*

"Antonio?" asked a white man who looked like Brad Pitt but wasn't. I nodded and shook his hand, couldn't remember what the woman at the table had said his name was. He pointed to a TV screen, and the translator—Abel, the only person in town who could speak English, though how well none of us knew—told me that's where they showed the footage we were adding sound to.

"It's an easy scene," Brad Pitt said, and Abel translated. "Mostly sitting, talking, drinking coffee. He patted me on the back. "Something to get your feet wet."

I looked at my shoes, wondered if I'd worn the right thing—work clothes with stains.

"We want to make it authentic," Brad Pitt was saying. "Use things that are native to your town. Dishes and fabrics and other materials. Leaves and dirt. Everything coming directly from here."

A few other guys walked in behind me. Turned out I was late and they were early. We would each be working on five-minute segments. Michael would show the movie on the screen and we would match the sounds with the things in the room. The chicken and steak and pillows were for fight scenes. Some of the carrots and tomatoes, too. The fabrics were for when the people on-screen moved around. It was supposed to be their clothes crinkling. But we wouldn't be using any of that today, Brad Pitt said. We were mostly going to be walking on the dirt from the roads in town and crunching some leaves with our hands. It didn't make sense to me why we were recording the sounds that had already been recorded, but Brad Pitt said it was because there was too much "ambient" noise. That wide-open spaces didn't have enough echo to catch small, crisp sounds on regular microphones. That we would be using special ones made for sound effects.

Michael's assistants set a couple of microphones by my feet and I spent most of the next hour walking in place, stepping on dirt from outside inside, at the same time as the people on-screen. I walked louder, then softer, or the other way around. I shook out sheets when the wind blew the tablecloths at Doña Tita's restaurant. They handed me coffee mugs and plates

I knew belonged to her and made me tap forks and spoons against them, scrape dry bread along the surfaces, tear some chicken with my fingers. And that was it. I had made more money in that hour than I made in a week doing repairs in town.

Brad Pitt patted me on the back. "A natural," Abel translated, though I could tell he didn't really mean it.

I couldn't believe my body, but it felt the way it feels when a woman you didn't think you'd ever have a chance with finally looks at you and doesn't look away. "Maybe I'll come work for you in Hollywood," I said.

Abel rolled his eyes but did his job and translated, "I don't see why not," then waved Oscar and Pepe over to the screen, ready to be rid of me. He must have heard the rumors about me and Patricia—his ex and one of the women in my rotation. I shook his hand as I left.

Outside, it was hot. Just past midday and I had an envelope of money in my hands. I walked home, past Doña Tita's, the restaurant in the scene I'd just been adding sound to. During the shoot, we were asked to stay away unless we were on set, but the film crew soon learned we weren't going to do that and just asked us to keep quiet. I stopped by wherever they were shooting for a few minutes every morning or afternoon, depending on the hangover, on my way to the church. Most of the town was doing the same and I would have to stand in the back and try to look over people's heads to see what scene they were shooting that day. The arrival of the crew had changed our daily routines, and everyone—the gossipers, the street vendors, even the old ladies with bad hips—was desperate to get in on the action. It seemed like the only person I never ran into at the shoots, not standing in the crowd or in the background of

a scene, not getting a crew member coffee or flirting with the
director, was Sarita.

She'd spent the entire week going about her usual business as
if what was happening was normal. She washed laundry and hung
it to dry in her backyard, she cooked meals for her parents and
Florencio, went shopping. The only difference in her schedule was
that the rooms at the hotel where she worked as a maid were now
always dirty and she had to go in more often. I guess, in that way,
whether from tips or the increase in her wages for the weeks they
were in town, she was also making money from the foreigners.

When I got back to my street, I saw her coming out of her
house and rushed the last few paces to catch her. "Look what I
got," I said, fanning out some of the bills in the envelope.

Sarita shrugged. "¿So what?" she said. "I got that, too." She
readjusted the basket on her hip and turned toward the market.

I followed after her. "¿What are you doing tonight?" She
didn't turn to look at me, but I was walking alongside her now
and saw the slight upturn of her lip. Yeah, I still had it.

"I have a date," she said.

I dropped the cigarette I had just lit and had to stop to pick
it up, then I jogged after her, sweat dripping down my back.
"¿Where?" I said, then spit out the dirt I'd failed to get off the
unlit end. "¿With who?" I said, and blew dirt off the filter before
taking another drag.

"That's none of your business."

I thought about everyone in town—old, ugly, married, or all
three. There were a few guys, but she'd never shown interest in
Tomas or Hector before. Maybe she was desperate.

"Manuel can't handle someone like you," I said, thinking
of the thirty-four-year-old widower. No children. Made good
money from the small liquor store he ran.

"It's not him," Sarita said. "His name's Michael."

"¿My kel?" Holy shit. Brad Pitt? The sound guy? He was like forty-and-some. He didn't even speak Spanish. How had they met? Had she already been in his hotel room? Had he been naked, coming out of the shower with his pink dick when she was there?

"¿You like that more than a real man's brown and thick?" I said.

"¿What?"

"¡You know what!" I said.

That asshole had had the balls to pat my shoulder and everything.

"¿You know what?" I said. "Whatever."

She stopped walking and finally turned to look at me. She looked angry but also sad, and I started to feel like she wasn't sad about herself anymore or about me but at me. I flicked my cigarette against the wall of Manuel's shop. I slicked my hair back with the sweat on my forehead and turned around without another word. I was stomping on the ground, and it sounded just like the noises I'd spent an hour on earlier. A few steps later, I turned to see if Sarita was following me, but she was gone, and so was the cigarette butt I'd smashed against the wall.

THAT NIGHT, I stood outside my house smoking, acting like I wasn't waiting on Michael and Sarita. It was dark and we had no streetlamps, so the only light came from the ember on my cigarette. I was on my fifth one and running low when one of those Jeeps that had pulled up at four in the morning a week ago stopped beside the one parked in front of my door. Michael stepped out in one of those James Bond suits and walked up to Sarita's door. He was about to knock when I cleared my throat.

"Antonio," he said, hand against his chest like he'd been expecting to see a jaguar. "The natural."

"¿What the fuck do you think you're doing at my door?" I said, taking another drag and stepping closer to him. The machete at my waist as hot as the cigarette.

He readjusted his tie. "Good work today," he said, attempting Spanish.

I exhaled, and before I could say another word, Sarita opened the door.

Michael turned to her and smiled. "Neighbors," he said. "*Vecinos.*"

"Very good," Sarita said. Her accent was thick, but the words were in English.

"You look *muy bonita*," Michael said, taking her hand and kissing it.

What the fuck was that shit? We didn't do that here. And for Sarita not to pull her hand back before his lips could touch her skin?

Michael helped her down the one-meter-high concrete slab that separated the front door of the houses from the road. He took her over to the passenger side of his car and opened the door for her, then closed it. "*Buenas noches,*" he said to me, then got in the car and drove off. Nothing but taillights and dust as he turned at the town square, then up the little hill that led out of town. Of course he was taking her somewhere else. Somewhere nice. Or, as nice as we had in the area. Probably down to Tangohuatchel, where the church roof was fixed before it started to leak.

I kicked my door, heard it rattle that metallic sound. It must have been loud, because Florencio came out.

"¿You okay?" he said.

"¿Where's he taking her?" I asked.

Florencio shrugged his shoulders. "She's been practicing her English, though."

I kicked my door one more time, then turned toward the bar. But no, who would be there? The usuals. And if Michael and Sarita went to bed, they wouldn't be coming back here, what with her parents and her brother. I turned back around and walked by Florencio, who was still standing outside his door.

"¿Where are you going?" he said.

"To the Americans," I said. "They have something that belongs to me."

Florencio shook his head. "That's your problem," he said. "You think someone can belong to you and that they'll be in the same spot you left them when you feel like coming back." I stopped in the middle of the road, no cars this late at night, and turned to face him. He was only sixteen but trying to act grown. "But people move," he said. "On, with, or away from each other. You have to choose who's going with you and hope they want to."

"¿You been reading Sarita's books?" I said. I could tell he'd been wanting to say this to me for some time now. Could imagine him practicing it in the mirror that morning. But Florencio only shook his head.

"Didn't need no book to teach me that," he said, then opened the door and closed it behind him.

I MADE IT to the hotel bar, where I never went because the prices were marked up. Could get the same *chela* at Milo's for half the cost. But I had extra money. And if Michael was going to try to sleep with Sarita, this is where he would bring her. I ordered a Gallo and a rum. Was sipping them when I felt someone standing behind me.

"¿Señor Banderas?" It was the woman with the clipboard and jobs from the first day.

I smiled at her. She'd remembered my joke. She said something in English, then signaled at the seat beside me. I nodded, pretended to dust it off for her, then waved around the air as if to say, *Probably not as clean as what you're used to.* She sat down and tucked a few strands of her shiny brown hair behind her ear. She'd brought her shampoo from the States. I could smell it.

The bartender came over, and she pointed to what I had and held up a finger. The bartender nodded and then set the drinks in front of her. He gave me a look like, *Hell yeah*, hermano. Normally, the bartender—in his washed-in-another-town work shirt and dried-with-a-dryer pants, with his combed-with-expensive-gel hair—would not say two words to me. He thought himself above most of us because he worked at the hotel. The two-story hotel with twenty-six rooms that looked like it had been dropped here from the sky. The one that saw fewer than fifteen customers a year. Most of those by accident. Travelers between somewhere and somewhere else, caught on the dark highway with no lights, just potholes and wild animals.

"Thank you," I said, nodding at the drinks, but we both knew what I meant.

The woman raised her shot, and I raised mine, too. "*Salud*," I said.

She wiped her mouth with a napkin, then said something I didn't understand. "Movie," she said.

Ah, that I knew. "Good," I said.

Some more words. Only one stood out: *Michael*.

I pulled at my beer, pretending to not understand at all.

The woman reached inside her purse and pulled out what I assumed was a phone. It was flat and rectangular. She pushed some things on the screen and then held it up to my face. There, in English and Spanish, were the words *My name is Janelle*.

"¿Janelle?" I said, with a hard *h*.

"Jah," she said. "Janelle."

I nodded. She handed me the device. It took some getting used to the small keys that were inside the screen instead of the buttons on a regular phone or computer, but I got the hang of it. And pretty soon, it was almost like we were talking. I would type, then take sips of my beer, look around for Sarita, then order us both another round. I would read what she'd written, what had been translated for me, then respond. A few more exchanges and another round. It didn't take long before we were laughing and drunk and I'd all but forgotten why I'd gone to the hotel to begin with.

That was, until I heard Sarita's laugh. Sarita had the most beautiful laugh. It was what I imagined two *quetzal* birds making love in the canopy under the morning sun sounded like. I looked over Janelle's shoulder, and there she was. Dressed in her nicest *corte*—with interweaving gold and blue strands running all the way down to her ankles. Tucked into the waistband, was the bottom seam of a tight-fitting, plain red V-neck top that made her little oranges look bigger than they were. She didn't notice me as I watched her follow Michael up to his room. I couldn't believe it. It had taken me months to get her into bed. And I was only the second man she'd been with. She wasn't like the women at the bar, but she was willing to be for him?

"Are you okay?" Janelle typed and handed me the phone.

I smiled at her. My I've-never-been-better smile. My I-can't-imagine-being-anywhere-but-here-with-you smile. "Yes," I said. A second ago, her hand had been on my forearm. Now it was in her lap. I took it in mine, kissed it the way I'd seen Michael kiss Sarita's earlier.

"I've never been inside this hotel before," I typed. "¿Can I see your room?"

She blushed a little when she read it. Yeah, I still had it. Maybe there was a little extra around my middle from all the beer. A little extra dryness from the cigarettes, from standing on roofs in the sun. But I still had most of my hair, if a some-what receding hairline. Mostly straight teeth. A little gold in there, but not too much.

She stood up, and I followed. The bartender walked over to our seats, but I shook my head. Made a little motion behind Janelle's back to let him know she'd settle the tab later. Gave him that don't-ruin-this-for-me look. The I'll-kill-you-if-you-open-your-mouth look. He nodded. He'd get the money later. He gave me a thumbs-up.

At her door, Janelle turned to look at me and said that thing I'd heard in all the movies. Of course the people who made the movies said what was in the movies.

Me either, I typed into her little device, then held it up for her to read. I kissed her on the mouth before she could say or type anything else. I shoved the phone into my pocket then turned the doorknob to her room, my other hand on the back of her neck. I led her to the bed, thinking about nothing other than how I was going to make sure Sarita could hear.

WHEN I WOKE up the next morning, Janelle was gone. Strange to feel trusted. Clothes in the closet. Jewelry and underwear that would fit Sarita in the drawers. Tempting, yes. But it would all be there when Janelle returned. On my way out of the hotel, I walked past one of the front desk workers, who must have heard about the night before and who shouted, "*¡El movie star!*" after me. I didn't stop, kept walking until I felt the sunlight.

Outside, I lit up a cigarette and looked at my watch. Didn't even have enough time to stop by the house and brush my teeth. I turned down the road, past my place. Wanted to peek inside Sarita's, but the curtains were drawn behind the windows. The iron bars that had always been there. Was it just me or did they now seem to hold a message specifically for me, like a sign hung on the doors of storefronts, a *sorry we're closed*, a *come back again soon*, a *you're not welcome*. I walked past the square, where vendors had set up their stands. The newness of the movie people was wearing off fast. The moment I walked into the studio, there was Michael, all you-know-what-I-did-last-night?

"Antonio," he said, a frown on his face. He pointed to his wrist.

I called the translator over. "Tell him I had a late night," I said. "Ask him if he knows Janelle."

Michael's frown deepened at the sound of her name. Maybe he'd tried with her before, but only I succeeded.

"He says to get into position," the translator said.

I walked over to where they'd placed a raw piece of meat on a platform in front of the microphone. Got on my knees for a better angle.

"It's from Don Omar's farm," the translator said. "For this scene," he translated for me, "you'll be matching a fight sequence. Each time a fist lands on skin, you punch the meat."

Michael played the scene a few times for me, then told me to start. The two *güeros* on-screen moved fast, but I tried to keep up. There was a fist to the face, then another. A kick to the ribs.

"Not there," the translator said. "We're going to use fabric and pillows for those."

"Start again," Michael said.

They played it back. I skipped the kick to the ribs. A kick to the face, and I punched the steak.

"Stop," Michael said. He paused the tape, ran his fingers from his temples to his eyelids, said something in English.

"He wants to know if you're drunk," the translator said. "You do smell like it."

I sucked my teeth. "No, asshole."

"Let's try again," Michael said, and the translator said.

Punch, punch, don't punch. Punch, don't punch. Then, on screen, a punch when two fists met, so I punched.

Michael paused the tape and got up from his chair, faced away from me.

"It was skin," I said.

Michael waved the translator over, whispered something.

The translator walked back to me, to where I was still kneeling in front of the meat. "He wants to know if this is about Sarita," he said.

I got up.

"Calm down," the translator said.

Michael turned to face us and, in very bad Spanish, said, "She told me all about you," followed by things neither I nor the translator could understand. When he noticed, he switched back to English and had the translator translate.

"Want her and every other woman. Want her only when it's convenient."

Who did this asshole think he was? I reached for my machete, and fear flashed in his eyes, in the eyes of the translator. I could have chopped off Michael's hands, but I put the still-sheathed machete down on the floor.

"¿Want to record some real fight sounds?" I said, fists up near my chest. I hadn't been in a fight since I was a teen. Back when my father started raising his hands to my mother. But I'd put a stop to that quick-like. A couple of knock-your-teeth-out punches, a few break-your-ribs-down-to-dust kicks, and he stopped. Left at night like some coward. I struggled to provide, being the new man of the house, and I must have taken too long learning how to make a living, because she followed him. Left no note or nothing. Went after what she knew wasn't good for her. Left me alone. Traded a family for bruises and eye shadow.

"Nah," I said, lowering my hands. "I know when someone ain't worth it." I stooped down and picked up the machete. Thought about kicking over the platform with the steak but didn't. I slammed the door to the house behind me. Saw the next group of guys coming to record some sounds. "It's all yours," I said, then patted Manuel on the back.

I jogged back the way I'd come, running between cars in the square. Almost bought a rose from Luis Carlos's stand but didn't want to spend the money or have time to haggle. I ran straight to Sarita's door. Showed up out of breath and sweating like an asshole in summer. I knocked twice, slicked my hair back. Realized I still hadn't brushed my teeth, but it was too late to turn back. I knew what I wanted.

The door opened. It was Florencio.

"¿Is your sister here?" I asked.

"¿Is everything okay?"

"¿Is your sister here?" I said again.

He looked me over while I tried to peer past him into the home. "Hold on," he said and closed the door behind himself. I heard him calling her name.

She came to the door with her hair in a braid. A white cotton blouse and her *huipil*. "¿What do you want?" she said.

"You." I gave her the all-I-ever-wanted-was-you look from the movies. The I'm-sorry-it-took-me-so-long look. She wasn't convinced, so I got on my knees, took her hand in mine like I had done earlier with the meat. "All I need is one more chance," I said. "I will never be with another woman."

"Get up," she said. "You're embarrassing me in front of the neighbors."

I stood up and looked around. Sure enough, people were leaning out of their doorways. Some were pretending to sweep their front stoops, but all of them were eavesdropping.

I looked back at Sarita. "Let them watch," I said, feeling like the hero at the end of the movie. "I love you." It's what they always said. I leaned in to kiss her, to take her in my arms, to highjack a Jeep and ride off into the sunset.

"You smell like sex," she said, putting her hand on my chest. She pushed me back and away, gave me an I'd-rather-kiss-a-pig look. A pigs-have-less-flies-than-you look. "Go home," she said. There was a sadness in her eyes. Then she closed the door, and I heard the lock. Loud as the gunshots they'd filmed last week.

I stood at the door for what felt like hours. Like I'd been standing there for centuries, forever. When I realized she wasn't coming back, I turned around.

"¿Still messing with her?" It was Luisa, the one with the big tits. Already drunk and off to work begging by the roadside. "Let me know when you want a real woman," she slurred, then shuffled on down the dirt path.

I turned back to Sarita's door and raised my fist. I could knock. Then I looked at Luisa. Ass like why-haven't-you-tried-this? Like not-love-but-something. I cocked my hand back but stopped. I kissed it and placed it on the metal door like, *Take your time*. I knelt on the pavement and listened to the sounds of the town—the birds, the church bell, people laughing, Luisa's bare feet dragging on the ground. I listened as her footsteps got farther and farther away. It sounded like hope.

SCRIMMAGES

―――――――――――

It was rumored that Salles Facundo, number 37 on the Guatemalan national soccer team, newly returned from a devastating loss at the FIFA World Cup qualifiers, was in search of a coaching job. We'd seen his performance on television—the missed goals, the failed blocks, the illegal tackles—and had been less than impressed.

"Guy kicks like my grandmother," Yuri said. "The one with the bad hip."

"Dribbles like a blind man on stilts," Mihuel added.

"Couldn't stop a ball if it was moving this slow," Jaramillo said, lazily kicking the ball toward Japito, who said, "Look, I'm Facundo," and kicked at the ball, missing it by half a meter. We all laughed.

"Sucks for whoever gets him as a coach," Yuri said, kicking the ball in front of him from center field toward the goal; it didn't make it even halfway there. "Whatever," he said. He picked up his Gatorade bottle and headed toward the locker room. We all followed.

A WEEK LATER, Superintendent Cornado came over the school's PA system and made the announcement. "There were four other schools bidding for him," Cornado said. "It was a close game, ¡but we got him!" He was gloating and would go on to tell anyone who would listen how he'd offered Facundo more money and how tuition would be slightly higher next semester but that it would all be worth it.

"And Mihuel's father gets a break this semester," Cornado said, referring to our current coach, who we knew hated the position and had only agreed to volunteer again because no one else would. "Replaced by a real legend," Cornado said, standing on the field with us the day Facundo was scheduled to start.

"¿Can't you ask another legend?" Yuri asked.

"¿One that doesn't suck?" Jaramillo whispered to the rest of us.

Cornado ignored us. "What this team needs," he said, "is a good leader."

But we had all stopped listening. Behind Cornado, getting out of a black pickup, was a man wearing Facundo's number. But it couldn't be Facundo. Even from where we stood, we could see the early stages of a beer gut that peeked out from under his jersey, the jowls like deflated balloons that hung where his cheekbones were so recently. We watched as this man, this imposter, wrestled a mesh bag of soccer balls from the back of his truck and made his way toward us, flicking his cigarette into the parking lot behind him.

"Mr. Facundo," Cornado said. "It's such an honor to see you."

Facundo nodded in Cornado's direction, sunglasses still on his face.

"This is your new team," Cornado said, attempting to fill the silence that had fallen over the field.

Facundo nodded again.

"Okay," Cornado said, "I'll let you get to it." He patted Facundo on the shoulder, then walked off smiling from ear to ear, like a schoolgirl who'd just been approached by her crush. We were sure he was never going to wash that hand again or was going to use it to masturbate.

Once Cornado was out of earshot, Facundo dropped the bag of soccer balls by his feet, reached into his pocket, and lit another cigarette. "You," he said, pointing at Jaramillo, "go get the cooler from my truck." He handed Jaramillo the keys in his pocket.

We all watched as Jaramillo ran across the field into the parking lot, watched as he opened the passenger door to Facundo's truck, then waddled back with the ice chest. "It's heavy," he said, setting it down by Facundo's feet.

Facundo tossed his cigarette onto the field, then reached into the cooler and pulled out a Gallo beer. He closed the lid—but not before the rest of us could see the nine or ten other beers inside—and sat on top of the chest, using his shoe to open the bottle in his hand. He took a long pull from it, then stared out into the horizon.

We all stood around and watched, unsure of what to say.

"¿Should we run some laps or something?" Mihuel asked.

Facundo shrugged. "If you want," he said.

We took off, just to get away from him, exchanging *He's crazy* looks as we ran. We stopped after a few laps and looked to Facundo, who said nothing, two empty bottles by his cooler.

"Maybe he wants to see that we're motivated," Japito said.

"I think he's just an asshole," Manuel said.

"Let's kick the ball around," Yuri said. "Show him we don't need him."

We got into two teams and began to scrimmage. About four minutes in, Jaramillo missed a shot and claimed the ball was underinflated. We argued about it but switched it out and started again. We ran a few more plays and made more attempts at goals, but anytime someone missed, they claimed it was because of their cleats coming untied or an uneven patch on the grass. The game went on like this for almost an hour, and when we finally looked up again to see what Facundo thought about a play where Samson was saying he'd been fouled, we realized he was gone. The only sign of him was cigarette butts and eight empty beer bottles.

WE DECIDED TO confront Facundo at practice the next day. We'd rehearsed it all during lunch and recess. We would say how we were paying him to be our coach, not to sit around all afternoon drinking beer.

"If we have to," Yuri said, "we'll tell him we're going to tell our parents."

"And if that doesn't work," Jaramillo added, jokingly, "we'll lie and say we like his playing style."

When we got to the field, however, Facundo was already there, soccer ball in hand, whistle hanging around his neck. "Line up," he said, pointing to center field. We did as we were told. "Yesterday," he said, "I saw you all struggling to breathe, huffing and puffing like you were dying." He walked up and down the line assessing what he was working with. "I bet you would have taken oxygen in through your assholes if you could have," he said. "That is a sign of the pampered," he said, adding that if we didn't learn to treat soccer as if it were a fight for our very lives, we would never play well.

Jaramillo raised his hand. "¿Isn't it just a game?" he said.

"For some," Facundo said, looking at Jaramillo as if he were a pile of shit served on a golden plate. Then he blew his whistle and told us to run until he said to stop.

We ran around the field for what felt like a small eternity, and with every few completed laps, Facundo would throw an empty beer bottle onto the field and tell us to speed up. Finally, after what could have been no less than one million laps, Facundo had us stop. "Line up behind a beer bottle," he said. We all stumbled our way to the six he'd flung onto the field.

"You must all make a shot from each of these six places before you can go home," he said. He dumped out all the soccer balls from his mesh bag and began kicking them at us, each one landing exactly where he intended it to go. "¡Begin!" He blew his whistle.

We all kicked balls at the goal half-heartedly. We were tired. We watched out of the corner of our eyes as Facundo looked at us, sipping on his beers and smoking his cigarettes. The sun had almost set, and we began complaining about how late it was getting and about how we could barely see the goal.

"Maybe we can bribe him," Japito said.

We looked over at Facundo.

"With beer," Jaramillo added, wiping the sweat from his brow with his sweat-soaked T-shirt.

But we ended up not needing to, because the next time Facundo reached into his cooler, we watched as he rummaged around the melted ice and came back empty-handed. He slammed the lid closed, then blew his whistle, instructing us to each grab a soccer ball and bring it in.

"Throw these away," Facundo said, tapping one of the empty beer bottles with his shoe tip. He turned to leave. "Oh," he said, "be at practice early tomorrow." He slung the bag over his shoulder, almost taking out Japito, and pulled the cooler to the parking lot, where he got in his pickup and peeled out like he was late for something.

"WE'RE GOING ON a field trip," Facundo said the next day. He'd had us walk to the employee parking lot, where he'd parked his truck, taking up two spots.

"We won't all fit," we said.

"I know," he said. "Follow me." He slammed the door to his truck, turning over the engine.

We followed his taillights, running past armed guards standing in storefront doorways, past police checkpoints, Pollo Camperos, and locally owned businesses. Past outdoor markets and mechanic shops, past chicken buses and city buses with *cobradors* hanging from doorways and heads sticking out of half-open windows, everyone staring at us in our uniforms as we inhaled exhaust from backfiring cars and motorcycles, then finally arrived at a soccer field two zones over, in Zone 15.

"You know there's one of these at school," we said. We looked at the patches of dead grass separated by dirt that made up the field. "A less shitty one," we said. "And unoccupied," Jaramillo added. There was a match going on—sweaty men in their late thirties and early forties, with chest hair like barbed wire and guts like small drums, playing shirts vs skins.

Facundo smacked Japito in the back of the head. "This is the problem with all of you," he said. "You're spoiled." He pointed at our fancy cleats and snow-white socks. "Too afraid to get your feet dirty." He pulled a soccer ball from the back of his pickup and told us about how he grew up playing without shoes. How his feet would bleed from broken glass in the field and how he'd have to go home to pull out pebbles that had lodged themselves in his skin.

"These men out here," he said, "are some of the best players I know. But they're too poor to play in a club, so they'll never be discovered." He began walking toward the players on the field. "Our national team is made up of people like you," he said. "That's why Guatemala has never made it to the finals."

We followed, unsure of what he had planned for us. "¿But didn't you play for Guatemala?" Yuri asked.

Facundo stopped without turning to look back at us and we all halted right behind him, hoping to stay out of arm's reach. "And you'll never know what I had to do to get there," he said, pulling out his pack of cigarettes. It was a vague answer, just like the one he'd given reporters when they'd asked him about his past, but we all knew the rumors. That Facundo had been in a gang and that's how he'd gotten the money to join the club where he'd been discovered. "But he doesn't have any tattoos," we said. People scoffed and waved their hands dismissively. "Money can make anything disappear." Another rumor was that his parents had moved to the States but had left him behind. In this story, his mother felt so bad that she'd send him money behind her husband's back—a few bucks here, a big sum there—and Facundo saved all of it, finally using it to pay his dues to the club. The stories made the rounds, came back sounding more absurd than when they'd left. We wanted to know more, could maybe trade the information for something we wanted later, but before we could ask any more questions, one of the men on the field whistled the game to a stop and waved at us. Facundo nodded back. He turned to face us. "You'll be skins," he said, telling us to take off our jerseys. We all looked around at each other uncomfortably. "¡Now!" Facundo yelled. "¡Go!"

We did as he said, shed our jerseys and ran onto the field. "Hello," we said, but the men ignored us. Yuri extended his hand for a handshake, but the man across from him placed a soccer ball in it instead. The men had us run laps, even though we'd just run kilometer after kilometer to get there. We passed the ball to one another, tried to keep it from them, took shots on the goal. Then, when we thought we couldn't run anymore, they had us play a scrimmage game against them. By the time the match was over, most of us were sure we had the pattern of the soccer ball imprinted on our guts or chests. We all got in a line to high-five at the end, glad to be done.

"See you tomorrow," the men called after us.

We sat or lay down on the grass, taking deep breaths, drinking from our water bottles, using our jerseys to wipe the sweat from our bodies. Facundo shook his head in disappointment, crushed his cigarette under his foot, then turned toward his truck.

"We need a break," we said, some of us puking into the ditch next to the field. They had pushed us harder than Mihuel's father ever had, harder than Facundo. Anytime one of us tried to call for a time-out, they ignored it; when Yuri tried to take a break by squatting down to catch his breath, one of the men pushed him over with his foot. There were no fouls either, just an ongoing slaughter that felt like a punishment in hell.

"Take all the time you need," Facundo said. But he kept walking. "Be safe getting home," he said. Then we watched as he got into his truck and sped down the street.

OUR PARENTS HEARD about Facundo's unconventional training techniques, said how strange they were, always adding, "¿But what do we know?" It was Facundo who'd gotten drafted to play soccer professionally, not them. Facundo who'd scored goals during Guatemala's CONCACAF Nations League qualifiers while they sat in their offices. So the day of the first game of the season, the turnout was bigger than usual. Jaramillo's parents had invited his aunt and uncle and their three children. Yuri's grandparents came. Even Japito's uncle was there.

"Just like we practiced," Facundo said, drinking from a clear water bottle, the beer foam spilling over the top. We got into position, called the coin flip, lost, then waited for the kickoff.

The weather was perfect, not a cloud in the sky, warm but not sweltering. Our jerseys were clean, looked better than the hand-me-downs on the other team, and our socks were as white as our teeth, no discoloration in either, unlike our opponents. The whistle blew and the game began. We had a few lucky breaks here and there, but the goalie was always faster than our kicks, diving like he had nothing to lose, not afraid to take a speeding shot to the crotch or neck. We didn't have that type of dedication, but we defended as well as we could: Japito, the natural leader of the team, took a few penalties; Nando strategized the corner kicks; we all made some throw-ins; and Mauricio secured a few headers. But no matter how well we did, the other team did better.

During halftime, Jaramillo asked Facundo if maybe we should concede as we searched through the cooler for the snacks he was supposed to have packed as the new head coach. The score was 4–0, and there was no way we were coming back from that. The other team could put in all their worst players and we'd still lose. But Facundo shook his head. "If this is really what you want," he said, "then you do not quit." Japito was still rummaging around in the cooler but found only more Gallos and a sandwich that Facundo had already taken bites out of. He pulled out a few ice chips and popped them in his mouth while Facundo looked on with disgust.

"¿Did you bring anything else?" Yuri asked, picking up the ham and cheese sandwich. Facundo snatched it out of his hand and threw it back in the cooler, then hauled the cooler back to his truck without turning back to look at us.

FACUNDO DIDN'T SHOW up to practice that Monday. And he didn't show up the day after that either. On Wednesday, we began to think it was our fault.

"Maybe it's because we didn't eat the sandwich," Japito said.

Mihuel's father got the call that night asking if he'd be willing to coach our team again—not permanently, just for the week. At first Mihuel overheard only one side of the conversation— the part where his father asked if everything was okay, then asked how much the bail was—then ran upstairs to listen in on the answers the moment he heard Facundo's name mentioned.

Turned out Facundo had been on a bender since our game that weekend, which had led to a fight, and had ended with him in jail. One by one, each of us got the news over the phone.

"Dumbass," Yuri said.

Then one of us—maybe Jaramillo—had the idea to bail him out ourselves. "¿What if we pay to get him out?" We all thought about this—what good would it do us to spend money getting out a coach we didn't even like? Then again, maybe he could put in a good word for us with one of the Guatemalan leagues and save us money in the long run. "Think of it as an investment," Jaramillo said.

"¿How much is it?" Yuri asked.

"My dad said he got the superstar discount," Mihuel said.

We imagined Yuri running the numbers in his head. "Lucky motherfucker."

Within the hour, we were all outside of our gated school building, some of us on bikes or skateboards or on foot, all of us with our allowances in our pockets. We hopped onto bikes, scooters, and mopeds and showed up at the police station, a bunch of thirteen-year-old kids with balled-up twenties and hundreds in our pockets and peach fuzz on our faces. After we'd finished signing the paperwork, Facundo was brought out from his cell and turned over to us.

"I'd offer to pay you back . . . ," Facundo said, trailing off and lighting a cigarette as we stepped out into the night. He blew the smoke in our faces, and we could tell he was still drunk—slurring and using our heads as stabilizers. His right eye was swollen shut and his nose looked crooked. He spat on the ground, and we noticed that the saliva was tinged with red. We looked into his mouth as he exhaled cigarette fumes, but all his teeth were still there. Then he spat again and we realized he wasn't slurring, he was lisping. We watched as he touched the tip of his tongue with his fingers and winced, and we winced with him, imagining it caught between the top and bottom rows of teeth as he got punched in the jaw.

"Don't worry about it," we said. We gave one another looks, silently arguing about who would ask Facundo if he still had any pull with the local soccer clubs.

But none of us had to ask, because Facundo took a long drag on his cigarette and started talking without any prying. "If it's not the money you want, it's a favor."

Maybe we weren't as hard to read as we'd thought.

Facundo sighed, then started walking, never once turning around to see if we were following. We, of course, were. It was then that Facundo would tell the story we would never ever, as much as we thought we would, tell our parents or friends or girlfriends, never tell anyone who wasn't there that day. Facundo started at the beginning, closing his eyes like he was traveling back in his mind, like he wanted to tell the story all at once. "I discovered my passion for soccer in middle school, fell in love with the sport and began playing after school every day, regardless of the weather—rain, heat wave, solar eclipse—and, pretty soon, I was better than most of the college kids I saw on the field.

"By the time I got to high school, I had my eyes set on a National League club; all I needed was the money—fifteen to thirty thousand spare *quetzales* a year in dues that my parents didn't have and never would. So I decided to get the money myself and took a job working at the clothing factory where my parents worked. But this ate into the time I would normally spend on the field. Nevertheless, I was determined, and spent the first two weeks practicing immediately after work, dribbling and shooting into the net well after sundown, when the only light came from the moon and the 24/7 grocery stores. But the routine became unmanageable. Even at sixteen, how could I be expected to go to school, then work, and still find time to practice? Either my schoolwork suffered or my skills did. I either got enough sleep or got enough practice, never both.

"After a few months of being stuck in this cycle, I gave up on my dreams of stardom and began looking for ways to cope. It didn't take long to find people just like me, who wanted more from life but couldn't find a way to get it and found themselves self-medicating—drinking, smoking, doing drugs, forgoing condoms, and playing with guns. So by the time my senior year came around, joining the club was the last thing on my mind. That is, until I got fired from the factory for not showing up, showing up late, or showing up drunk.

"The manager told me it was the owner's decision and that he was just following orders. I yelled at him to get the owner, told him to tell the owner to be a man and come fire me face-to-face. But the manager only shook his head in disappointment and got my parents to escort me out. My parents said it was a miracle they hadn't gotten fired as well and maybe it was for the best that I had, that maybe I could focus on going to university. But I couldn't let it go. I'd given up my dreams to work there. Now not only did I not have a job, I still didn't have the money for the club and I didn't have the skills to run the field anymore, all of it washed down the drain with beer and long hours spent at the factory. I swore revenge and bided my time.

"Six months later, after working my shift at Pollo Campero, I left work to pick up my parents at the factory, where I saw the owner exiting the building and getting into one of those sleek and shiny cars you only see in movies. I don't know what came over me, but before I knew it, I was parked outside his house. A house not far from where you all live."

Facundo stopped at a four-way street and threw his cigarette into the middle of the road. He lit another and then crossed. All of us followed.

"I got high that night, grabbed my gun, and returned to his house to rob him of everything he owned. I was loading up a pillowcase with things that looked expensive when the lights in the living room came on," Facundo said. He turned left down a street with no lights and none of us hesitated for even a moment before continuing. "It all happened so fast," Facundo said, leading us across the street without checking for traffic. He walked through the middle of the next street like he was sleepwalking, then got back on the sidewalk. He didn't say anything else for two blocks. He didn't have to; we could all imagine the next part—the reach for the gun, the smell of dinner still in the air, the sound of a bullet lodging in a throat.

A block later, Facundo started talking again. "The story was all over the news," he said. "There was no way to sell the stolen goods that soon, but I still quit my job and got back to practicing. I spent months getting back in shape and waiting. I couldn't believe how long it took. People get shot in Zones 1 and 2 every day," he said, "but we never hear about that on TV. Yet the factory owner's face was in the headlines for longer than I could have imagined. Eventually, though, the news cycle did move on and no one was ever charged with the murder. That's when I managed to sell the items—some heirlooms, some gold earrings, and other shit I couldn't understand anyone owning: Guatemalan Civil War memorabilia, expensive cuff links, fancy-looking rings. I used the money to pay my dues and join the club.

"Y'all know the rest," he said and flicked his cigarette against a wall. But we didn't. We were overflowing with questions—why had he played so poorly after getting drafted, and had he started drinking before or after that showing? Why hadn't he been traded to Mexico? Had he killed anyone else? We continued following Facundo, our minds racing, but before any of us could manage to ask anything, Facundo stopped walking, and we all bumped into him, stepped on the back of each other's shoes. Facundo sighed. "This is me," he said and pointed at a nondescript building along Avenida Quatro—nothing like what we imagined his home to look; it was barren, no soccer posters, no Guatemalan flag, just a black door and bars on the windows. We looked up at the terrace, where we could see clean laundry blowing in the wind.

"Be at practice early tomorrow," Facundo said, crouching down to pull a key from a small hole in the concrete of the stoop outside his front door. He didn't turn to look at us or give us time to process what he'd said before he turned the key in the lock and opened the door to his house. Facundo stepped inside and shut the door behind himself before we had a chance to realize that in our hunger for Facundo's story, none of us had bothered to grab our rides or suggest that we all take the bus. We surveyed our surroundings—the nearly empty streets, the sound of drunks and *eloteros* echoing in the alleys—the sweat coming from our bodies. We thought of knocking on the door, of asking to use the phone to call our parents, but we knew it would only lead to questions. Instead, we retied our laces, started our walk back from where Facundo had left us.

THERE WAS SOMETHING different about practice the next day, like it was full of possibility or imbued with some kind of meaning. Facundo showed up in his old soccer outfit—same socks, same cleats, the number 37 jersey—but there wasn't a beer or cigarette in sight.

"¡Line up!" he yelled, and we did as we were told. "Today, you get new positions." He said he'd been watching us play, that he knew our strengths and potential. "Don't argue," he said, then called out who was goalie, who would play midfield, who would defend. "Let's go," he said, then blew his whistle. There were a few grumbles, some murmurs—why did Japito get switched to the left side, when he was right-footed? How was tiny Samoro going to stop anything from getting between the posts? We looked at each other but did as he said.

We scrimmaged for two hours, with Facundo stopping the game to ask us what had gone wrong with each play, what we could have done differently. "One eye on the ball," he said, "one on your teammates." He blew his whistle and told us to start again. "¡No!" he'd shout, or, "¡That was worse, do that again!" He handed us bottles of water, talked to us about how to watch our surroundings and the field as a whole. "If you don't watch the field, the other team will steal the ball and be gone before you know it."

We spent the rest of the week doing drills—short and long passes, shots on the goal, running plays. "Today," he said, "corner kicks." We all lined up, half on the left side of the field, the other half on the right, and practiced curbing the ball, mostly sending it flying in a straight line, despite our best efforts. The day after, we took penalty shots. The sound of the ball against the goalposts could be heard echoing in the stands of the school field, with only the occasional goal. Finally, on Friday, he taught us how to pass and move, pass and move; how to keep our heads up; and how to misdirect. We ran into each other, colliding, bruising our thighs and bloodying our noses.

Facundo seemed less than impressed with our progress, but by that Friday evening, we felt like we could take on the world.

We clapped each other on the back, our hands making loud smacking sounds, leaving imprints on sweaty shoulder blades.

"Take a knee," Facundo said, signaling at the ground around him. "Tomorrow," he said, rubbing his temples, "we have another game." We elbowed each other in excitement. There was no way we could lose, and we said so.

"Gonna kick some ass tomorrow," Yuri said. We all cheered.

"A round of applause for Facundo," Jaramillo said. We all clapped and whistled.

Facundo held up a hand, calling for silence. He opened his mouth but then stopped himself from saying whatever it was he was going to say next and looked—really looked—at each of us. We waited as he stared into each set of eyes, saw us as individuals: Mihuel the future banker who loved Cantinflas movies, Jaramillo the painter and father of two, Abel the older brother, future wife beater, and insurance agent. He was looking at us as Yuri the future debate team captain, Casimalo the future politician, Bendito the future gangbanger. Not a professional soccer player among us.

Facundo sighed, stood up from his kneeling position, and wiped at his shorts. "Be early tomorrow," he said, then collected the soccer ball at his feet and turned away. It was, to say the least, less than we had expected from our final pregame pep talk, but we chalked it up to Facundo being tired from actual coaching or cranky from withdrawals. But nothing was going to bring us down. Not the traffic on the way home from school, not a significant other spotted holding hands with a classmate, not even the thought of losing. We were invincible as we ate our dinners, did our chores, watched TV, masturbated in the shower. We fell asleep that night dreaming of a victory we had never known—one we had earned ourselves.

THE NEXT MORNING, we were on the field thirty minutes early, stretching, doing warm-ups, looking around for Facundo, who seemed to have forgotten about the game, as the scheduled kickoff time came and went without any sign of him. "Just a few more minutes," we said, thinking he had relapsed but would be there any second, hungover, maybe holding a beer, but there nevertheless. Even Mr. Cornado, who'd come to cheer us on, was hopeful and had gone so far as to call Facundo's neighbors to ask them to knock on his door. Then, even though we pretended not to notice, we watched as he dialed the number to hospitals and the nearby jails.

More time went by, in which all of Mr. Cornado's searches turned up nothing. Finally, tired of waiting, the referee told us that we either played without Facundo or forfeited the match.

We were set to give up, but Mihuel's father came down from the stands and said he would lead the team one last time. He put us in our old positions and placed two fingers in his mouth to use as a whistle. He rotated players from the bench to the field like we were cards in a game of poker, but none of us said anything. We played distractedly, always keeping one eye on the ball, as Facundo had instructed, but the other we kept on the stands, as if Facundo might walk up at any moment to coach us to victory, to repay us for bailing him out of jail. Eventually, we figured he wasn't coming, but it didn't stop us from looking up at the stands anytime we caught the whiff of beer from an uncle's flask or saw a flash of light that we mistook for the cherry of a cigarette.

We lost, and when the game was over, we walked off the field and waved half-hearted goodbyes to one another. We played the rest of the games that season not caring if we won or lost—it wouldn't change the trajectory of our lives. Some of us would move on to high school, others would drop out. Some of us would immigrate to the U.S. while others moved to small towns outside the city or down into Honduras or up to Mexico. Still, sometimes we would think back to that last practice, how when he thought none of us were paying attention to him, Facundo would juggle a ball low to the ground using only the tops of his feet, how he would do the beginnings of a rainbow kick but stop himself from completing the motion. We watched as he controlled the ball at his feet like it was a part of him, wired like the rest of his body to do what he told it to.

We'd see each other in the hallways and nod or give each other fist bumps, but it was never the same as when we were a team, especially not after we saw the death announcement in the newspapers:

Salles Facundo, 32, survived by a country who loved him. A great soccer player, friend, and coach. He will be missed.

And that was it. No cause of death, no further explanation—not even from Mr. Cornado over the PA system. We speculated about a drug deal gone wrong, a bar fight with knives, alcohol poisoning. We circulated stories about how the factory owner had survived the gunshot and come back for revenge; how Facundo had sold all his belongings and bought a one-way ticket to the States; how he had faked his death to avoid having to see us lose our final game.

But in the end, none of us ever really learned the truth, or if we did, we didn't know it. We went on to marry and divorce and have children and vasectomies. We fell in and out of love with life, used our savings on vacations and expensive cars, none of us ever really leaving our gated school building, none of us every really doing anything worth mentioning, except maybe being able to say that once, a long time ago, we knew someone like Facundo. And even now, one of us will sometimes remember him, and the rest of us will feel it—the way the atoms in the air will change, become charged with potential, then turn into nothing; the way the moment passes and we find ourselves slightly disoriented, wondering how we got to the grocery store or how long the car behind us has been honking; the way we slowly regain our bearings before answering the next question on our children's homework assignment or replying that no, we don't want cheese on that. How strange to still be finding our way back from where Facundo has once again left us.

HOTEL OF THE GODS

Twelve cabins. Each of them given the name of a Maya deity. We had Acat and Hun-Chowen for the creative types, Acan for the drinkers, Ekchuah for the short-term stayers. Then there was Mulac, Kan, Ix, and Cauac, after the gods of the four winds, which sat farther into the jungle or along the road on either end of the hotel premises; Chac-Uayab-Xoc up near the lake; Ixazalvoh for female travelers; and Hobnil for families or the wealthy. The last cabin, Xbalanque, was mine. It wasn't much different from the rest, except I'd put in a television and a window unit. I also had a mosquito net around the bed and was thinking of installing a water heater.

I was on my way out when I saw headlights coming down the road, past the piers along the lake, the public outhouse, and the closed-down taco stand that used to serve soggy tortillas. I was hoping the driver was lost or finding a place to make a U-turn, mostly because I was hungry and wanted to make it to Tita's for a *shuco* before it got too late, but the car kept coming, stopped directly at the entrance to the property.

"¿Got any rooms left?" We were enveloped in darkness and I was blinded by the headlights, but the voice was unmistakable.

It was my brother, Ignacio. He was drunk and leaning against the open door of his car.

"¿For who?" I said.

Ignacio spat on the ground, then cleared his throat. "Gabriela kicked me out," he said.

"¿Again?"

"For real this time," he said.

She kicked him out "for real" at least once a week. If it wasn't because of his drinking, it was because she found lipstick on his shirts or drugs in his pockets.

"Someone just booked the last room for tonight," I said.

Ignacio looked at the row of cars parked along the bank, did some mental calculations.

"I just need it for a few nights," he said. He spat on the ground again. "It's half mine anyway." There was a begging in his tone that he was trying not to let me hear, and he shuffled the dirt around his feet to cover it up. He only ever got like that when he was really drunk. Otherwise, it was fuck Gabriela and fuck her house and fuck you, then off to bed, but right then, he looked vulnerable, maybe even lost.

"¿Can I use your car in the morning?"

Ignacio looked at his car—a piece of shit he claimed was vintage, American even, as though I couldn't see the Toyota logo on the trunk—then rubbed the hood of the Corolla before saying yes.

We walked back to the reception desk, Ignacio stumbling behind me.

"¿When are you going to fix these potholes?" Ignacio asked. They hadn't been there when Dad owned the place. I hadn't known they were ever a problem.

"It's because you're drunk," I said. "Everyone else navigates them just fine." I walked behind the reception desk, which sat under the cabana near the middle of the property and afforded a 360-degree view of the cabins surrounding it and the jungle surrounding them. It was where I spent most of my time, listening to the monkeys and birds call out to each other.

I got him the key to Acan. "Trade," I said, holding out my hand for the keys to his car.

He hesitated, weighing his options. I could see his mind working, almost like a movie: car, gravel road, or hotel bed? He sighed. "Be careful with it," he said, then dug them out of his pocket.

"Don't worry," I said, handing him the room key. "I won't drive it while drunk."

He looked at the name etched into the Caribbean pine the key was hooked onto. "Very funny," he said, then turned down the path toward his empty cabin.

IN THE MORNING, I took Ignacio's car for a joyride. I had nowhere to go. Just tired of going from sitting in my room to sitting behind the reception desk, like I lived in a cage. I left the customers to figure shit out on their own. Most of them had other places to be anyway, and those who didn't could ask Ignacio for whatever they needed. I didn't care. The hotel had been our father's dream, not mine, but I'd still spent my childhood summers carting around cleaning supplies and plungers. Dry towels and bedsheets. All of us cramped in Ekchuah, the smallest cabin, leaving the better ones for the customers. Year in and year out, we rented rooms to guests while Ignacio and I slept on the floor, our parents sharing the bed. And the place stayed afloat. Looked nice, even.

Now I was letting it sink into the ground. Had no idea how to run a hotel but was somehow stuck with it. Mostly because by the time our father died a couple years ago, Ignacio had his own house, a wife, a kid; and I had back problems, nothing else to show for my twenty-four years on earth. Not even a scar. No addiction. No legacy.

"You don't know the value of things," my father used to say anytime I complained about cooking dinner for customers. "Look at this grill. Step outside and look at the view." He never seemed to notice the burns on my forearms, the mosquito bites on my legs.

About ten kilometers down the road, still in Ignacio's car, I pulled into an empty embankment along the other side of the lake. From there, the hotel looked like scattered pieces of firewood. A couple of alligators swam along, probably scared off by the gravel crunching under the tires. That was the farthest I ever got from the hotel, even as an adult. The school me and Ignacio went to as kids was one kilometer in the opposite direction of the property. The convenience store was at the end of the road that led down to us and the lake. Even the weekly food markets took place along the main highway that ran between the small restaurants and houses in town. I'd had my first kiss at the crumbling church, behind the altar. Snuck a girl into one of the cabins when I could. But the girls were all grown and gone now. Even Ignacio had left and come back when the outside world got to be too much for him. But me, I'd had a whole life's worth of experiences here, along the banks of that lake. And when I died, I'd be forgotten, just like everyone else in town. Disappear just like the ripples left

behind by the alligators that were swimming farther and farther away.

WHEN I GOT back to the hotel, there was an angry customer sitting
at one of the tables in front of the reception desk.

"You're the guy who checked us in," he said. "I've been
knocking on your door." He stood up, his fists clenched at his
side.

"I wasn't in," I said.

The man frowned more deeply, pointed a finger at me and
said, "¿You been out fuckin' some cows?" He pointed toward
the fields in town. "¿Fuckin' cows instead of running your
business?"

"It's not *my* business," I said.

The man took a step toward me, and I walked behind the
counter like there was important paperwork waiting for me
back there.

"I want my money back," the man said, taking another step
toward me.

"But you've spent the night." I checked my clipboard like
I didn't already know—two adults, one child, came in around
ten p.m., requested a late checkout, staying in Mulac.

The man slammed his open palms onto the counter, but
before he could say anything else, a voice cut through the
echoing sound of flesh on wood. "¿Killing mosquitos?" It was
Ignacio. He was standing at the edge of the cabana, sweaty
and covered in what looked to be dirt. I looked back at the
man, watched as his eyes made their way down to what Ignacio
was holding—a shovel. His other hand on the hilt of the
machete tucked into his belt.

"We paid for water," the man said, not looking away from the shovel.

Ignacio pointed at the lake. "¿How much more can you need?"

The man took in a deep breath and puffed out his chest, then took his hands off the counter and faced Ignacio. He looked like he wanted to argue but thought better of it and exhaled, deflated. "We're never coming back here," the man said. He didn't turn around but walked to the edge of the cabana still facing us. When he was no longer standing under the same roof, he turned around but looked over his shoulder a few times as he made his way into the jungle to get his family.

"You're letting the place go to shit," Ignacio said, walking over to the counter.

I looked at him. "Not like you're doing much to help," I said.

He smiled at me. "¿Don't you want to know why I look like this?" He waved his hand in front of himself. His pants were frayed near the bottom and at the knees; his plain white shirt looked like spilled coffee. There was dirt in his hair and on his face.

"I don't see anything different," I said.

He shoved my face with his dirty palm, the same way he used to when we were kids, smooshing my nose like he wanted me to lick his hand.

"Asshole," I said, pushing his arm away.

Ignacio wiped his hand on his dirty shirt. "Come on," he said, then started walking without turning to see if I was coming.

I followed him up into the jungle, through the foliage with no path. Nothing but dirt, sticks, leaves, bugs. No stones covered in muddy footprints, just untrampled ground. We were walking adjacent to the other cabins, back by Cauac but farther west. I was getting scraped by branches and eaten by mosquitos, but I didn't say anything, was going to follow Ignacio until he stopped. When we finally reached a clearing, somewhere I don't think I'd ever been, not even in my childhood, I noticed that there were some recently chopped branches along the outer edge of the opening. And a hole.

"¿What do you think?" Ignacio said, spreading his arms wide and spinning slowly in a circle.

I had sweat dripping into my eyes, so I wiped at them with the back of my hand, like maybe I was missing something. I opened my eyes and took another look around.

"It's nice, ¿right?"

I looked around again. The way he was acting, you'd think Ignacio had found a door to Xibalba or an alternate reality, but all I saw was the same thing I saw every day—trees, rocks, birds, except these were other trees, other rocks, other birds. Maybe the hole had magical powers.

"¿Is it a shitter?" I asked, pointing at the hole. It was about the size of a toilet seat. "Like, ¿does it make your shit disappear or something?"

Ignacio stopped spinning and lowered his hands to his side. "¿Why would I be building a shitter all the way out here?" he said.

I shrugged my shoulders.

"I'm building another cabin, you idiot."

I looked at the hole. "¿For mice?"

Ignacio bent down and picked up a handful of freshly dug dirt and threw it at me. He bent down for another.

"Stop," I said, raising my hands in surrender. "I was just kidding."

Ignacio let the dirt sift through his fingers and I mussed my hair to get it out, dusted it off my shoulders. Then we stood in silence as the particles settled, both of us staring at the hole.

"She really kicked you out, ¿huh?"

Ignacio nodded. Wiped nonexistent sweat from his nose with the back of his forearm. "I was thinking we would name it Hunahpu."

One of the Hero Twins. I knew because our father was obsessed. When he wasn't running the hotel, he was reading up on our past, the one we had back before the conquistadors. He would sit us down with the *Popol Vuh* and the Books of Chilam Balam, made us memorize over a hundred gods, and taught us some basic phrases in K'iche'. Our mom had left him because of it. She was raised as a good Christian and would not buy into false prophets, no sir, not her. The one thing the conquistadors had done right was to bring us their true God, the benevolent savior, the son of man, amen. She left when I was fourteen, when our father began spending his free time in the jungle surrounding the hotel, building us each a totem of our Maya spirit guide. He'd walked in one day with a slab of wood carved to look like Mulac and set it on the small table next to their bed, right above where my and Ignacio's heads would be that night.

"Jesus Christ," our mom had said.

"Mulac," our father corrected.

She was gone not long after that. The only good thing that came out of it was that me and Ignacio got to share a new room when we weren't full, mostly so our father could grieve in private.

"¿Do you know *how* to build a cabin?" I asked Ignacio.

"With your help," he said, signaling at an extra pair of gloves and one of the shovels we used when we were kids. They were leaning against one of the many trees I hadn't had a chance to notice yet.

I shook my head. "Go ask her to take you back," I said.

Ignacio frowned. "It's not like that this time," he said, then stabbed his shovel into the ground. He grunted and pushed it in with his foot, then dug out a pile of dirt and set it next to the hole.

"¿Where do you even find other women?" I asked. He must have been driving to one of the bigger towns. Seemed like a waste of gas to me. I guess I was lucky, because the one good thing about the hotel was that I never had to go anywhere; women came to me. Stopped on their way to a better place because our cabins were cheaper or because they got caught driving the lightless highway at night. Or they wanted a short vacation, somewhere with a lake. Maybe they couldn't afford a place somewhere else. Whatever their reasons, the lake and I were always waiting.

Ignacio stopped digging for a moment, then faced away from me. "It wasn't me who found someone this time," he said, then drove the shovel back into the ground with such force, I was sure the handle would break.

"Shit," I said and watched as Ignacio wiped away at his face. Maybe at the sweat or maybe his tears. I didn't know how to make him feel better, so instead I asked him why he didn't just take one of the other cabins.

Ignacio shook his head no. "That's for the customers." He dug the shovel back into the ground.

"They're usually not all full," I said.

"¿And you don't think that's a problem?" Ignacio spat. The anger in his voice, if I hadn't been looking at him, I would have thought our father was back from the dead. "We're going to get this place back to the way it was."

For what? People still came. Why mess with what was working? I spat on the ground. "Don't drag me into your punishment," I said, walking back to the check-in desk.

"¿Don't you want to get out of here?" Ignacio called after me. "¿Aren't you tired of doing the same thing every day?"

I spun around to face him. "¿What does restoring this place have to do with that?" I asked.

"We can sell it, Javier. Leave this place."

I looked into his eyes more closely. He was six years older than me but looked at least ten years older from all the alcohol that had added the deflated tire around his waist. He really did look like our father. Maybe I did, too. "¿What's so great out there that you ended up coming back?"

Ignacio looked at the ground. "I'm going to do it right this time," he said.

I didn't believe him. He had no idea how to do that. I didn't either. "Whatever," I said and walked away. I gave him another hour before he went into town to get drunk. I could almost hear his car starting and the crunch of the gravel. Could almost smell the alcohol on his breath, feel his weight under my shoulder as I helped him toward his usual cabin again.

THE NEXT DAY, I checked people in and out as usual. Cleaned the rooms, changed the sheets, swept the floors free of bug carcasses. But this time, I also stood on a chair and wiped the spiderwebs from the corners of the ceiling, brought out the mosquito nets that moths had eaten through to sew together the salvageable parts.

Ignacio had spent the whole day in the jungle the day before, walking to the desk only to grab more water from the kitchen—

wide enough for one person and a spatula—in the back. He was out there even after the sun had set, and I knew he couldn't see shit anymore but was just trying to make a point. Either that or he'd snuck to the bar in town without me noticing. Whatever the case, I'd woken up right before sunrise to check on the hole, but even before I'd gotten to the clearing, I could hear Ignacio's labored breathing. I didn't let him see me, but I watched as he continued working. He was covered in sweat, and it was clear that he'd either been there all night or had woken up early to keep going.

"¿Want some?" Ignacio was standing knee-deep in the hole, which now took up a decent size of the clearing. It was close to noon now, and I was holding half a torta out to him.

He turned his back to me and drove the shovel back into the ground.

"Fine," I said, then sat the edge of the hole and dangled one foot in, the other tucked under me. I took another bite. "¿Shouldn't we be focusing on the other cabins instead of building a new one?" I asked through a mouthful of food.

"Hunahpu-Gutch," Ignacio said without turning to look at me. "Not the other twin." He shoveled more dirt out of the hole.

That's when it clicked for me. Ignacio wanted to change the cabin names so that each was named after one of the gods of creation. There were thirteen of them; that's why he wanted to build one more.

"Hopefully we can get it right the second time," Ignacio said, referring to the fact that it took the gods three tries to successfully make humans, the dry earth and mud version destroyed by water, just like the humans made with wood.

"¿You're not gonna build the cabin out of corn, are you?" I asked, remembering the third, successful attempt at creation.

Ignacio looked up at me, his face stone-still. Then he started laughing. I laughed, too, and for a few seconds, it felt like we were kids again.

WE SPENT THE next few months cutting down trees for the new cabin, spreading concrete for the foundation, and nailing support beams for the roof, as well as sprucing up the other rooms. Bought new sheets and blankets to make up for the old mattresses, put down rugs to hide the discoloration of the floors. Then we carved the new names of the cabins on scraps of wood and hung them above each door. When we were close to done, near the beginning of April, we made two signs with the new name of the premises—Hotel of the Gods—which we'd carved into the trunks of two trees and painted yellow and blue to make them stand out. Ignacio drove one of the signs thirty kilometers down the road in one direction and the other thirty kilometers in the opposite direction. When he got back, he cracked the first beer I'd seen him drink since we'd started the project.

"I thought you were done with that," I said.

Ignacio took a long pull from the can and pretended to misunderstand what I'd said. "We are," he said and signaled at all our hard work with his hand, the one holding the beer, his other hand wrapped around my shoulder. He finished his drink in two long gulps and crushed the can, letting it fall to the ground beside him.

"Help me with this," he said, heading to his car and opening a back door. I peered through the window. Inside was a giant sign advertising Gallo beer.

"¿Where the fuck did you get that?" I asked. The seats in the car were pushed up as far as they could go to make room for the monstrous lettering and rooster head I was sure could be seen from outer space.

"Grab that end," he said, opening the other back door. He began pushing the sign, which began sliding out of the car. If I was going to avoid cleaning up broken glass, I was going to have to help. I lifted my end and waited for Ignacio to come back around to help me pick it up.

"They give them to you if you agree to carry their product," Ignacio said, bending over to help me lift.

"¿How much did you agree to carry?" I said, straining under the weight of the sign.

"It'll draw a younger crowd," Ignacio said, pushing the sign so that I had to walk up the hill backward. "And they'll spend their money here instead of at the restaurants."

I adjusted my grip along the edges. "¿Is that the crowd we're going for?" I asked.

"¿The kind with money?" Ignacio said. "Yeah."

We set the sign down on the reception desk.

"I could use a beer," Ignacio said. "Sign's working already." I helped him lift it onto a small wooden table he set up behind the desk. It protruded slightly into the doorway leading back into the kitchen, which I thought was a fire hazard, but which Ignacio said wasn't a concern. Then he plugged it in and flipped the switch.

"Shit," I said, covering my eyes. When I opened them again, Ignacio was smiling. His face was lit up blue from the neon, and I could see splotches of green on his neck and forehead, his teeth as white as could be.

WITHIN THE FIRST couple of weeks, guests were coming in saying they'd seen the sign Ignacio had set up on the road and did we still have rooms available? It was completely different from before, when people would take one look at the hotel and, unless they were dead tired, get back in their cars and drive the extra hour to get to the next major town, where they would pay twice as much for a place to stay. Now word was spreading about what we'd done with the place, and the locals were no longer ashamed to recommend it to tourists. It was getting to the point that we had to do something even our father had never had to do—turn people away due to a lack of vacancies.

"At this rate, we're gonna have to build one cabin for each god," Ignacio said, counting the money we'd made at the end of the first month. We'd even taken to rooming together again—me on the bed, Ignacio in a hammock, snoring the way only drunks do—to open up the newest cabin for customers.

Then we'd spend our mornings and afternoons cleaning shit off the floor and vomit off the walls for the next group of people who were coming in to make the same mess the following night. I didn't even know about the buy-two-get-one special Ignacio was running on beer until someone pulled up to the hotel, walked up to the reception desk, said they'd seen the announcement under the signs Ignacio had set up along the road, and asked if it was true.

We'd upped the price of the rooms and charged a cleaning fee the customers were free to get back if they let us inspect their room before they left. The few older travelers who did that had begun to dwindle and disappear altogether by the end of the first month. They would pull up, take one look at the Ping-Pong table and Solo cups, the trash that littered the ground when we didn't have enough time to clean it all up, the half-naked people sunbathing topless or bottomless—Ignacio among them—and turn right back the way they'd come.

Ignacio spent his mornings sick and woke up only because I would open the window and door to let in the air and let out the smell, or splash him with water, which he then had to use to clean the piss from under his hammock. He wanted to hire someone to help but didn't want to spend any of our income, scared he wouldn't be able to afford the next case of beer, the next key bump straight from the capital that someone offered him.

One night in the middle of June, I was trying to get some sleep, but Ignacio was pulling another late one with the newcomers. I could hear his voice above all the rest, could see the neon lights from the sign sneaking in through the cracks in the window. Finally, when I couldn't take it anymore, I got up and walked to the reception area, where empty bottles and cans lay across all the tables. Ignacio was laughing loud enough to scare owls and wake jaguars, his arm around a blonde who was struggling with her Spanish. Whether from the beer or her nationality, I couldn't tell.

Ignacio spotted me before I could ask to speak with him privately. "¡I'm so happy you're awake!" He winked at the blonde. "We were hoping we could use the room," he said, pinching her thigh.

"It's almost three in the morning," I said.

"We won't be there all night," Ignacio said, and the blonde giggled and nuzzled her face into his neck.

"We need to establish a curfew." The whole room went quiet.

Ignacio looked at the guests' faces, how quickly their smiles had dropped. "He's just kidding," he said, but no one believed him. Even the blonde who had just been sucking on Ignacio's ear leaned away from him. Ignacio turned back to me. "Get me another beer," he said, all the slurring gone from his voice. "Now."

I shook my head. "It's my hotel, too," I said.

Ignacio scooted back the bench he was sitting on so hard that the blonde he was sharing it with almost fell off and had to hold on to the table to steady herself. "This," he said, both arms outstretched, a beer in one hand, "is not the same hotel you used to own." People were shifting uncomfortably in their seats. Some of them were laughing quietly, others whispering. They'd never stayed at a place like this. "The one you owned was barely staying afloat," Ignacio continued. "Now get me and my friends another beer." It sounded like a line from a bad movie, but maybe that's why it worked. All the people sitting at the tables, one by one, began to chant for another drink.

"¡A round on the house!" Ignacio shouted, and everyone cheered and pumped their fists in the air. Some clapped Ignacio on the back. And the blonde was on his arm again. Looking around, I knew this wasn't the time. I would let him have his fun that night and come up with what to do in the morning, when Ignacio would agree to anything as long as I left him alone to nurse his hangover, so I turned to leave. "¿Where are you going?" Ignacio called after me. "Get us our beers." I kept walking, and that's when I felt something fly right by my ear. It was Ignacio's beer bottle.

It landed in the kitchen area behind the desk. Some people gasped, but soon, their shock was replaced by laughter. I turned just in time to see another bottle coming at me, this one thrown by one of the drunks at the table who thought this had turned into a game. I ducked, and the bottle kept going, not into the kitchen this time but directly into one of the many neon signs Ignacio had since acquired, this one advertising Corona on the wobbly table behind me. Upon contact, the lettering exploded into pieces and sparks and beer rained down onto the outlet where we plugged in the beer signs and the lights that ran along the side of the cabana. Electricity crackled. Then the cabana caught fire.

"Shit," Ignacio said. He grabbed a few half-empty bottles of beer and stepped over the bench. He tripped and would have fallen if it hadn't been for one of the pillars holding up the cabana. He righted himself and ran past me, behind the desk, and turned the bottles upside down. The fire was like his anger—the moment the alcohol touched it, it raged harder. "¡Fuck!" Ignacio yelled. He stomped on the flames, but they were already making their way up the wooden walls and into the palm leaves on the roof. "¡Help me!" Ignacio yelled at no one in particular, but I couldn't move, and I guess no one else could either. We watched as Ignacio slapped at the wall with his hands, but it was no use. More and more of the roof began to light up and smoke.

Finally, a few of the others got up, but not to help; they were running out from underneath the flaming roof, which had begun to collapse in segments. Others followed, all of them screaming, until there was no one left inside but me and Ignacio.

"¡Do something!" Ignacio shouted. But what was I supposed to do? The place hadn't been rewired since the day our father built it. There was no stopping the fire from leaping from one bad, rusted wire to the next, or from one old, damaged banana leaf to another, since we hadn't replaced the roofing—something our father had done every three years.

"Come on," I said, grabbing Ignacio by the arm and leading him out of the cabana. The people who'd been in their cabins also stood outside now, making their way down the paths or watching from their windows. I was sure that even the people in the cabins we couldn't see were watching the flames grow taller and taller. But why were they going higher and farther if the cabana was almost burned to the ground?

"We have to get the buckets from every room," I said. I turned to the crowd and told them to take the buckets down to the lake and fill them with water. People began running to their cabins, and me and Ignacio did the same. We fumbled around with the door and turned on the lights, then got the bucket I'd placed next to Ignacio's hammock in case he needed to throw up and the one we'd placed under the sink. Outside, I ran to the back of the cabin to grab the orange one I'd set up to catch rainwater, but when I got back to the cabana, Ignacio and I were the only ones holding buckets; everyone else was holding their stuff.

People dragged suitcases and carried loose clothing items. Others held keys and shoes. They all ran past us, half clothed, half awake, but stopped short of the water, getting into their cars instead. Over the sound of crackling wood, we heard the sound of engines turning over and the sound of dust being kicked up by the exhaust pipes.

"Fuck," Ignacio said. "¡Fuck!" He threw his bucket to the ground and kicked it. Then, an afterthought. "The money," Ignacio said. He stared into the flames where the reception desk with the profits locked inside it had stood.

"Forget that now," I said, holding him back, seeing the look in Ignacio's eyes like he wanted to run back in for it. "Help me." I handed him a bucket and then began running down the hill to the lake. What would normally be dark and unnavigable now shone bright with the light of the flames.

I made it down to the lake and filled the bucket, then ran back up and threw the water on the trees that hadn't yet caught fire, hoping it was enough to keep the flames from spreading. Ignacio was right behind me, stumbling over the potholes we also hadn't fixed, and the empty beer bottles left behind by people who hadn't cared enough to clean up after themselves. Then we both ran back down and filled the buckets again, but the fire didn't care how determined we were.

We ran from one god to the next, dousing the perimeter in water and stomping on the edges of the fire until there was nothing left of our shoes. We ran until our lungs burned, as if we were eating the flames instead of putting them out. We ran. And at some point, the light moved from the earth to the sky in the shape of the sun. But we couldn't stop running down to the lake for more water, almost like a proverb.

DARK ROAD WITH DIESEL STAINS

Lorraine wants the kid to go with me. To hang out, eat up, sleep in, the window, fast food, the cab.

He wants to spend time with you, Lorraine says. She's cornered me in the living room—cheap furniture, faces north, has about nine pallets' worth of square footage, the biggest room in the house.

With the loads right now, I say, I don't know when we'd be back.

Not that it matters during the summer. But it's better than admitting the truth: I don't want the responsibility of having him with me.

Lorraine turns to look at Milo, who's sitting on the couch with headphones on. He's either nine or ten years old now. Almost-black hair, just like mine. Almost darker-skinned from playing in the front yard with no sunscreen.

Without another word to me, she speaks loud enough for Milo to hear her over his music. Grab your suitcase, she says.

Milo screams, jumps off the couch, and runs to hug me, his head near my belly button.

I shake my head and pull him off me, have no idea when he grew so attached. Last time I saw him was almost a month ago, and the time before that it had been at least three weeks. Both times, I couldn't have been here for more than twenty-four hours before I had to get back on the road. It's been like that since he was born. Up until he was six, he probably couldn't've picked my face out of a lineup. Now he wants to go on a cross-country delivery with me—an almost-stranger.

Come on, Lorraine says. Milo nods and runs to the back of the two-bedroom, where I can hear him opening his closet. Lorraine follows, and I check the time. If we leave now, we can beat the traffic. Otherwise, I'll have to lie in my logbook to make up the difference.

Let's go! I shout, then go into the bathroom to take another leak. Gotta make sure I get it all out before we begin the drive. I wash my hands, look in the mirror at my thinning hair, my beer gut, the dark bags under my eyes, then turn off the light and go sit on the couch.

A few minutes later, Milo's dragging his Teenage Mutant Ninja Turtles suitcase down the hallway.

Finally, I say, and check the time again. We're late.

We drive to the empty lot of what used to be a Sears—the only place large enough to park the truck but where teens have been known to hang out and skate. So while Milo and Lorraine unload the car, I walk to the back of the trailer to check the locks. I'd found them bent or stripped a few times and had heard about drivers who woke up in their cab to the sound of bolt cutters and people unloading the semi-trailer.

I check the air pressure on the tires—all eighteen of them—and make sure the mud flaps are still on. No holes or dents in the fuel tanks, and nothing's crawled into the exhaust stack. I climb into the cabin and already Milo's jumping on the bottom bunk bed, the top one still in the wall.

Don't do that, I say, then pull out my logbook. Lorraine's sitting in the passenger seat, and it almost feels like we're a family, but then she says, What's this? and holds up a baggie with my stash in it.

Back before we were parents, we used to snort it on weekends. Even tried to heat it up with a lighter and aluminum foil once but ended up almost setting the carpet in our apartment on fire. Then we'd found out Lorraine was pregnant and agreed to stop altogether. But every now and then someone would have it at the bar, and I couldn't help myself. My slipups hadn't seemed like that big of a deal to her back then, before the hospital bills and diapers and formula. Before I began driving for J.B. Hunt to pay the mortgage on a house with space for the baby and a backyard for when he's older.

It's not mine, I say, then look back at the logbook to avoid her stare.

You fucking liar, she says softly enough so Milo doesn't hear. You promised me.

I tried to explain it to her a couple of months ago after I'd left a baggie in my pants pocket, which she'd found while doing my laundry. She'd sent Milo to the neighbors', then tried to get me to agree to NA, and nothing I said—how I needed the coke to stay awake during overnight hauls, how I couldn't afford to lose time by having to stop every few hours to piss out coffee—made her back down. So I'd lied, said I would look for meetings while on the road. She'd ask about them sometimes, and I'd show her tokens that I'd bought at truck stops that I thought looked like sobriety chips. Now, with the bagged powder in her hand, I fall back on the excuse I'd used when I'd agreed to go to meetings.

Wouldn't it be worse if I fell asleep behind the wheel? I say, reaching for the baggie she moves out of reach.

She doesn't say anything, turns to Milo instead. I love you, she says. Enjoy your time with Daddy. And something about the way she says it makes it sound like there's a finality to it. Then she climbs down the steps on her side of the truck and slams the door shut behind her. Soon, she's in the car and speeding away, running a stop sign like she can't get away fast enough, like seeing me once a month is too much for her.

And I have only a second to wonder if there was a specific moment in our history when our relationship started going to shit before Milo runs to the front of the cabin and says, What are these? He shoves the latest issue of *Penthouse* in my face with one hand and my *Black Hawk Down* VHS tape with the other.

Give me those, I say, snatching the items from him and shoving them into one of the overhead storage compartments. Go, I say, then turn over the engine. While it warms up, I write in the logbook, check the map to make sure I know the route. My usual haul is from Tallahassee to San Diego. Before that, when I worked for CFI, I drove from Queens to Little Rock. Now they got me driving down to New Orleans or Tulsa or any other place they feel like. This load is heading up to Pittsburgh. And it's in a refrigeration trailer, so it's probably frozen dinners and ice cream. But what I'm really checking is whether there's a place I know between here and there where I can stop to re-up. I have cities all over the country circled. Love's and Pilot and TA locations where I can stop to shower and score.

Where are we going? Milo says, peering over my shoulder.

I close the map. Sit down, I say.

Can I sit up front?

Yeah. Maybe if he sits up here now, he'll ride in the back after we make a stop in Memphis. Buckle up, I say.

He climbs onto his seat, raises it so he can see over the dashboard, and I turn on the CB to channel 19 and push in the air brakes. That hissing sound more familiar than my own voice.

BY THE TIME we get to Memphis, I'm ready to rip my ears off. The kid hasn't stopped asking questions since we left and there's no sign of him letting up. Every time a voice comes over the radio, he has a question about what's said. *Who's Smokey Bear? What's a henhouse? I didn't see no alligator.* I don't want to explain that they're code for cop, weigh station, and popped tire, afraid there'll be a follow-up. I opt for telling him that I don't know or that he's misheard the announcement. Truth is, I'm too busy watching out for the cops and trying to avoid a flat. Especially in the south. The police here are ruthless. And the roads are full of potholes.

The Love's where I scored last time is off the next exit, so I ignore him when he asks me how much the truck weighs. Seventy thousand pounds would mean nothing to him anyway. I flip my turn signal, follow the signs for the gas station, and park next to a pump. I still have enough gas to get me to Louisville, but I might as well fill up to avoid another stop later.

Can I come? Milo asks.

I tell him no.

But I'm bored, he says.

I slam the door closed and lock it, walk to the passenger side and lock that one, too, not that he can't open it from the inside. I prepay for the diesel, then walk into the store. I look around for a second, buy the kid a soda so I don't have to hear him whine, then exit out the other side. I bum a cigarette from another driver, ask him if he's seen any action. He tells me someone's around, then nods toward the back. I thank him, puff on the cig, and pretend I'm minding my own business.

When I turn the corner, I see him. He's unmistakable in his uniform: baggy jeans, snapback, oversized shirt. He's sitting at a picnic table, smoking a Black & Mild, so I lean against the building and push with my hand like I'm checking the architecture. When he notices me, I tilt my head up and he does the same. I walk over and stand off to the side of the table.

¿Qué pasa, amigo? he says.

I pull out the hundred- and fifty-dollar bills I'd folded and put in my pocket when I left the truck.

He nods and tells me to sit down at the table, then reaches into his pocket. And in that moment, I feel like I can see into the future: the smooth movement with which he'll give me a handshake that takes the money from my palm and leaves behind the eight ball, the walk back to the truck, where the pump will have stopped and the kid will sit with his face pressed against the windshield. But when the guy looks back up, his arm stops halfway to mine, then his hand retreats back into his pocket. He looks over my shoulder and nods upward.

That you? he says.

I turn, and there, looking like a past version of myself, is the kid.

I look back at the guy. It's all good, I say, but I can tell that it's not. The guy shakes his head, then stands up to leave.

I'm just trying to stay awake, I say, extending the money as covertly as possible.

The guy looks at my hand and lets out a small chuckle. Aren't we all, he says, then flicks his cigarillo into the parking lot like, *Get your shit together*, like, *Don't be an asshole*, like it's him standing back there, not me.

It's not like that, I say, but he just keeps walking.

I pocket the money and turn back to the kid, who's standing there lost. I walk back to him but throw the pop in the trash can before I reach him.

Was that your friend? he says.

I turn him back toward the way we'd come by pushing on his shoulder. Why aren't you inside the truck? I say.

I got scared, he says, and looks at his shoes as we walk. I open the door to the Love's. There was this woman knocking on the door, he says.

I stop, look at him, and then look over the aisles toward where I parked, check my pocket for the keys. It was probably nothing, I say. A Jehovah's Witness.

We exit the shop on the other side, where I immediately notice that the kid has left my door open. As we get closer, I can see through the windshield that the microphone coax cable isn't hanging where it should be. I quicken my pace, and the kid runs behind me. I reach the cab and pull myself up onto the seat, but I don't have to look to know the CB radio is gone. Not even the mount is left. They took it all without removing the screws.

I look around the lot, but I know they're long gone. I check the back, and the TV is still there. Probably too heavy to carry. I check for the mini-fridge and for a second, my hand can't find

it behind my seat, but then it's there. I open the glove compartment, but it's empty. I'd almost forgotten that Lorraine had
already robbed me of what was in there. Then I reach up to the
storage compartment above my seat and feel around, but I can't
find nothing. Gone is my *Penthouse*, gone is the VHS tape and
my logbook, but I still have the money I'd taken out from between its pages.

Can I get in now? Milo calls up to me. He's standing in a
watered-down oil spot.

I let out a deep sigh and lean my head back against my seat.
He starts to climb up the stairs. Take off your shoes, I say. He
does, then tries to climb over me, but I push him away, step
down to let him get in, then close the door behind us.

Can we get something to eat? he says.

I ignore him and push in the air brakes. Then I reach for
the CB out of habit and my hand goes through thin air, but I
can almost feel it. Kind of like when people talk about phantom
limbs. I shift the truck into first and we lurch forward with a
jolt. I'm making the turn onto the highway when I see the diesel
pump nozzle sticking out of my fuel tank. It slithers along the
side of the truck like a snake with its fangs sunk into the metal,
and I waste no time in pulling over to remove it.

WE STOP FOR the night at a rest station right outside of Nashville,
where we brush our teeth, take shits, and eat from the vending
machines. We're walking out the double doors when the kid
spots a pay phone and asks if he can call his mom. With the
last of the loose change in my pocket, I dial Lorraine's number,
and pretend not to be listening to see whether or not she asks for
me. Pretty soon, I forget why I'm standing outside the booth.

There's sweat on my forehead and under my armpits, even though it's cold outside, and it feels like my head is full of radio waves, like someone's trying to reach me from somewhere but they can't get a signal. I wipe at the sweat with the back of my forearm and look up at the moon. White as white. Nothing but moondust and rocks up there.

Here, Milo says, bringing me back down. He's leaning out the small booth, holding the phone out at me. I hand him my bag of chips, suck the Dorito cheese off my fingers.

Hello? I say, taking the receiver from him. Hello? I say again when Lorraine doesn't answer.

If you wish to continue this call, please deposit twenty-five cents.

I dig around in my pockets, but they're empty. I check the coin slot and the top of the phone, but no luck. I'm about to tell Lorraine I'll call her back when the phone begins to beep beep beep like it's trying to rush me off. I hang up the receiver and open the door to the booth. I want to ask the kid why he didn't tell me the call needed more money, but when I step outside, he's not there.

Milo? I say into the emptiness around me. Nothing but the hum of trucks on idle. I walk back up to the entrance of the building and can't see him through the glass, so I go inside. I check the nook with the vending machines, in case he's gone back for more snacks. Then I go into the bathroom and call out his name. All I hear is grunting, then the plop of shit hitting toilet water.

I walk outside again and think of shouting his name, but I don't want to be dramatic. I jog to the back of the building, where it's nothing but woods and the sound of cars driving by on the highway, and turn back around. I'm halfway across the lot when I hear someone call out to me, but I ignore her.

Hey! she shouts again.

This time I turn to look. It's a white woman in her mid-forties, her teeth crooked and stained.

I'm not interested, I say. I know the type, with her faux-leather thigh-high boots and platinum-blonde box-dyed hair with dark roots showing. I turn back toward my truck, but she calls after me again.

Fuck you, not interested, she says. *I'm* the one's not interested. She stops a few feet shy of me. Just thought you'd want to know where your boy ran off to, she says, digging in her purse for something.

Where? I say.

She nods her head over toward the building. By the picnic tables, she says, lighting her cigarette.

I squint in the darkness, looking toward the other side of the building.

He's playing with my dog, she says, then exhales a cloud of smoke so perfect, it looks like it'll make its way straight up to the sky and stay there.

Thank you, I say.

Mm-hmm, she says, sucking on her cigarette again. Come on.

As we walk toward the outskirts of the woods, I remember that time in Guatemala with my parents. We'd landed in the capital, where we boarded a chicken bus, then another, then a van, and finally, after two days on the road, reached the foot of the mountain where my father had grown up. We slept in hammocks, and the next morning, my father shoved me awake. He put his finger over his lips, then instructed me not to wake my mother and to put on my shoes. He handed me a machete and told me it was about time I learned how to use one, then began walking into the jungle. We walked for what felt like months, and when I couldn't take another step, I stopped and told my father I needed to get the dirt out of my shoes. He nodded and said he was going to hike up ahead to check the trail, then left.

I sat on the hard ground, leaves strewn around me, above me, beside me, everywhere. Finally, I stood back up. Only twelve years old, but my muscles screamed like the monkeys I'd heard in the trees all morning. I walked the way I'd seen my father go, but I couldn't see him. ¿Dad? I said, quickening my pace, feeling like something—one of the jaguars or javelinas my father had told me about—was watching me behind every tree. ¿Dad? I broke out into a sprint, tripped, got back up and kept running.

I never did find my way out that day, and hours went by before my father finally walked back for me. He shook his head, told me America was making me weak. That when he was a kid, his father had done the same thing to him, and that he'd found his way home on his own, had killed a rabbit and taken it back with him to present to his father. But look at me, worse than a girl. Then he turned and walked away without looking back at me.

When we arrived back at his childhood home, only my mother ran out to meet me. She was crying almost as much as I was.

¿How could you do that? she said, spitting at my father. But he just kept walking.

He would have found his way back if you'd let him, he called over his shoulder.

And I don't know why I did it—maybe out of pride or shame or both—but I pushed my mom's arms away from me. I just needed more time, I said, then followed my father up to the house. The satisfied smile on his face almost made it worth it.

When we get to the side of the truck stop building, there's
Milo, sitting on the ground with a little gray and white dog in
his lap.

Look, Milo says, petting the dog as if I can't see it.

Let's go, I say, grabbing him by the arm and forcing him to
his feet, the little dog scurrying away, then stopped short by its
leash.

Can *we* get a dog? Milo says.

Thank you, I say to the woman.

She nods, takes a drag on her cigarette. I'm staying here,
too, she says, waving vaguely at the parked trucks. Her dog
sniffs at my leg, then walks to the other side of the table, where
it squats and begins taking a piss.

Okay, I say. Thanks again. I push Milo toward the truck,
unlock the door, tell him to get inside. I slam the door shut
behind us, then go into the back of the cab. I open the mini-
fridge to look for beer, but there's only an open one, and I don't
know how long it's been there. I pull it out and sniff it. But half
a beer—especially a flat beer—won't do anything. I put it back
and climb into the front. It's too far to Louisville without the
cocaine, and it'll be even farther tomorrow if I don't get a fifth
or a six-pack to calm my nerves tonight. Maybe I'll even get
lucky and find someone selling at the next stop, but I'm trying
not to get my hopes up.

I thought we were staying here? Milo says when I turn the
engine over.

Buckle up or get in the back, I say, releasing the air brakes.

Aren't you tired? he says.

I turn on the headlights.

I know *I'm* tired, Milo says.

I floor the clutch.

I told Mom we were staying here tonight, he says, and his voice makes it sound like the gears are grinding. She asked if you were feeling okay. I turn to look at him, can't tell if he's lying, and have no time to ask because then he's screaming and pointing out the windshield. My eyes snap back to the lot just in time to see the woman and her dog standing right in front of my grille.

Shit! I slam on the brakes without pushing the clutch, and the engine goes dead. The truck wobbles like we ran over something, then everything goes quiet. I'm scared to look, but I finally stand up a little and lean over the wheel just as the lights flick back on. I expect to see nothing but emptiness, but there's the woman and her dog.

She moves out of the way of the headlights, and flips me off. Fucking asshole! she shouts up at me, then bends down to scoop up her dog. Fuck you! she shouts, middle finger still in the air, then disappears into the shadows of the idling trailers.

I sit back down on my beaded seat cover. My nerves are shot to shit and I can feel myself shaking, all the blood gone from my extremities.

That was so scary, Milo says.

I go into the back and pull out the flat beer, chug it in a few gulps, then put the crushed can back in the mini-fridge.

I'm glad the doggie's okay.

I shake my head violently, put the stick in neutral, then turn the engine back on. The air brakes are already off, and the lights are still on. I press on the clutch, then check both side mirrors. I look out Milo's window, then look out of my own. There, in the light from one of the open doors of a truck, is the woman and her dog. She's talking up to someone in the cab who I can't see, who must be leaning down to hear her over the engine. I see the woman say something, then nod and tie the dog leash to the pole that helps drivers climb the stairs, leaving the dog outside. A man sits up and scoots over to the passenger side, allowing the woman to climb inside. When she shuts the door behind her, the lights in the cab go off, and all I can see is the reflection of my truck in his windshield.

Are we going? Milo asks.

And I can't say why, but I unbuckle my seat belt, leave the door open as I run over to the dog and unhook it from its leash. But it doesn't move. Looks up at me as if it's expecting something. Go, I say, making sure I'm not heard inside the trailer. Go! But it just stares. That's when I lift my foot and kick it with enough force to send it flying under the trailer, where it whimpers and yelps as it hits the inside tires. As soon as it gets back up, it takes off running in the opposite direction of where I came from, and I run back to my truck, where Milo is waiting.

We hit the highway, and it's so quiet, I can hear the road underneath us. It stays like that until I'm pulling off at an exit forty-five miles away, when I think I hear the dog as the wind blows past us. I look over to see if Milo heard, but he's just staring out the window, so I check the sideview and can almost imagine a wolf with its muzzle turned upward, howling at the sky.

WE PARK IN the Flying J lot. The engine has barely turned off before I'm rushing the kid out the door and into the store, because I can't remember what time they stop selling alcohol in Tennessee. We make it to the cooler section, and I grab a twelve-pack of Coors and an eight-dollar bottle of wine. No liquor in sight. At the cash register, I give the woman my ID and the cash. She's ringing me up when the kid walks up behind me holding a candy bar.

Put it back, I say. I expect him to argue, but he doesn't. Then when I turn back to the woman, she's shaking her head, almost imperceptibly, but I can tell she's judging me for not getting him the chocolate. I'm going to get him real food, I say, and she gives me a courteous smile and hands me the receipt. I snatch it, then put my arm on the kid's shoulder, making sure the clerk sees, and lead him to the Arby's. But the line is so long, and I can't wait any longer. I reach in the bag and pop open a beer.

You can't drink in here, the cashier calls out.

I pretend she isn't addressing me and look over my shoulder, but there's no one there, and the woman tells me to get out or she'll have to call the cops. Whatever. I hand the kid a five and tell him to get himself something, then walk outside.

I'm smoking a cigarette I bummed from another driver when the kid comes out holding a paper sack. I've just cracked open my third beer, having chugged the first two, the alcohol mixed with the nicotine calming my nerves.

I got you some fries, the kid says.

I take the last drag on the cigarette and flick it against the wall. I'm not hungry, I say, then lead the kid back to the truck. As soon as I pop open another can, a tractor I've seen before pulls up to one of the pumps. It's rare to run into other truckers you recognize, but it happens, and I'm hoping whoever it is might sell me a line. But when the passenger-side door swings open, the woman from the truck stop forty-five miles back steps out, and I almost spit out my beer. I turn off the cabin lights and scoot down in my seat. I'm hoping she won't notice my truck.

Is that the woman from earlier? Milo says, pointing.

I pull his arm to hide him from view.

He rubs at it and asks why we're hiding.

Because I'm an idiot. I should have known better than to stop at the very next place that had room for eighteen-wheelers.

We're not, I say, then I peek over the steering wheel and watch as she yanks the door to the station open and charges inside. I set my beer in the cup holder, then tell Milo to put the rest of the cans and the wine in the mini-fridge as I start the truck.

We drive for over an hour, crossing into Kentucky, but I don't have the strength to drive on to Louisville. I've been pulling the truck back from the sleeper lines for the last half hour, so the beer is working its magic. I decide to pull over on the side of the road. Something we're not supposed to do but that cops will excuse on occasion. Especially since I have the kid with me.

It's late, and when I look in the cabin, the TV is on, but the kid's asleep. He's on the bottom bunk, hidden under the covers. I open the mini-fridge and pull out two more beers and the bottle of wine, unscrew the top and tilt it onto my lips. The leftover fries and part of the sandwich sit in the bag on the passenger seat. I lean over and shove them into my mouth, then reach for the CB but remember it's gone. I open the glove box, as if the baggie will be there, then close it, wipe the sweat from my palms on my jeans, tilt my head back, and pour more wine inside.

I don't know when it happens, but I fall asleep, and when I wake up, it's to the tapping of something on my window. I open my eyes and there's a flashlight in my face. I shield myself with my arm and accidentally tip over the empty bottle of wine. Shit. I look out the window again but can't make out who's on the other side.

Officer, I say, moving one of the beer cans from the cup holder to the passenger-side floorboard.

The voice on the other side of the glass finally comes into focus for me. Roll it down, it says.

His breath is fogging up the window, so I reach for the crank, but then there's another flashlight on the other side of the truck. I squint against it and can finally see through the windshield. A third person is lying on the hood of my tractor.

What the fuck? I say, and I think I'm saying it into the microphone the guy at my window is holding out at me, but it's not a mic.

Get out, the guy says, and I realize it isn't a cop hat, a badge, a nightstick. It's a ski mask, a reflection of the light catching the gold of a wristwatch, and something more dangerous than a nightstick.

I reach for the ignition, but the keys aren't there.

No, no, the guy on the hood says, then cocks the gun.

I raise my hands.

Unlock it, the one at the driver's-side door says.

I reach for the door handle and barely get it open before the man's hand snakes in and pulls me to the ground by my shirt collar. I land on the asphalt, scared I'll be hit by a car, but the highway is dark, not a single person driving by.

Where are the keys? Someone has pulled me to my feet.

They should be in there, I say and am quickly pistol-whipped. It hurts less than I expect, but the blow knocks me back to the ground.

Check his pockets.

Someone picks me back up and reaches into my pocket and I hear the jangle of keys.

Let's go, one of them says, then they're rushing into the truck.

Wait, I say, but they're not listening. One of the guys runs to the back of the trailer and I hear a car door open and close, then the sound of an engine turning over.

I walk, dazed, back to the open door of the tractor, but it slams in my face. I reach up and pull on the handle, but it's locked. I bang on the door. Hey! I shout, then start beating on the side of the trailer where the bunk beds are. Wake up! I'm shouting.

The car parked behind the truck peels back onto the highway, honking its horn in victory.

I'm still banging on the trailer when it lurches forward, almost running my foot over. I step back just in time to hear the truck shift into second, then I move out of the way as it merges onto the highway. I think of running after it, grabbing the locks in the back and hoisting myself up to the roof until the truck stops, when I'll jump down and surprise the thieves, tell them they can keep the load but I want the kid back. But that's something that only happens in movies.

It's only ice cream and frozen meals, I say, not loud enough for anyone to hear even if they were around.

I'm watching the lights on the trailer as they grow more and more distant. They're almost around the next curve when I see the brake lights come on. I watch in the darkness, but I think I see the passenger door open and something fall or get pushed out. I start running toward it, but I think of my father and that time in the jungle and stop myself. Maybe Milo will grow up to be stronger than me if he can find his way on his own. The truck takes off again; I can hear the exhaust coughing out of the pipes, and in the reflection of the taillights, I think I see the figure standing up in the darkness, but I don't move. I watch as the figure looks around, then the truck is gone and we're left in darkness again.

I hear what I think is the word *Dad*, but it's so distant, I can't be sure. *Dad?* I hear again and again, but I can't respond in words. Instead, I tilt my head back as far as I can and howl or scream or yell, up at the stars and the cloud of smoke the woman at the truck stop blew up there. I do it again, then look back at the figure of the kid up ahead, expecting him to be getting closer. But he's not. I howl again, but the sound of his voice is growing softer and softer.

He's scared of me, doesn't recognize the sound of me reaching out for him. I try again, but the outline of his body is growing smaller and smaller. It's then that I realize that my voice probably sounds like danger. And he's running in the opposite direction.

A CLEANSING

At first, women wouldn't bring me their underwear. They'd start with a blouse, then move up to skirts. Only when they saw what a good a job I did, how I removed stains no one else had been able to get out, would they bring me their undergarments. I was a *lavador,* the only one in our village and possibly all of Guatemala. It was seen as a woman's job; a job that cracked skin and drew blood from palms and knuckles, that caused wrist and back pain, shoulder and leg pain. Basically, it was a job for the desperate, and I was no different.

I'd started washing clothes ten years earlier, as penance for something. I couldn't quite say why, but I had the vague sense that it helped. People would drop off their baskets or handheld piles—once, even a garbage bag of clothes by some American tourist passing through—and I would get to work, kneading and scrubbing, then twisting and squeezing. I would hang the items to dry on the clothesline outside and hope for sun. Lastly, I would iron and fold, spray them each with lavender perfume and send them on their way. It was hard work, but it was also a routine, one I had no interest in disrupting. So when the girl showed up at my door, I wanted to tell her no.

"¿*Who* sent you?" I asked again. I thought she was lying.

"Señora Magdalena," she repeated. She was dressed in boys' clothes, had tearstains on her face and pigtails in her hair. "As soon as I showed up at her front door."

"¿And she sent you to me?" I looked up and down the cobble-stoned street.

"She said you wash clothes."

I looked at the girl more closely. She couldn't have been older than thirteen. "¿Where are your parents?" I asked. She didn't answer, only extended a sheet of paper she pulled out of her pocket, but I couldn't read, and neither could she.

"¿Do you want to wait inside?" I asked. She nodded, wiped her feet at the door.

"But I don't think they're coming back," she said.

I offered her the only things I had to eat: *pan dulce*, some beans, and a chicken from earlier that week, all of which she turned down. "If you change your mind," I said, and left a plate for her on the counter. A storm was rolling in, so I needed to get the orders from the clotheslines and bring them inside.

"¿Where are you going?" she asked.

"To work," I said.

"¿Can I come?" She followed me out back, keeping a few paces behind me until we reached the sunlight disappearing behind the clouds. "Wow," she said. She was watching all the linens and shirts blowing in the wind. I had bedding from the local hotel hanging up to dry along with a few orders from my neighbors. "All that white," she said, reaching out for one of the bedsheets. "It looks like heaven."

I got to work on the clothespins. "If you're just going to stand there," I said, "go inside."

She came over and I started handing her the pins, filling baskets, hampers, and laundry bags with the clean items some-one else was going to get dirty all over again. "If you overpack them without folding them first," I said, "they start to wrinkle." I laid the sheets in as loosely as possible so that they wouldn't start to crease or take shapes that I would later have to work harder to iron out.

We got everything off the lines and inside right before the rain began. The rainy season was always the worst time for busi-ness, because customers would take their laundry to *lavanderías* with electric dryers to avoid any delay in getting their clean clothes. But those places didn't offer the care I did, the attention. I hadn't lost even a sock in over eight years. Not to mention that I was within walking distance, unlike the bigger places all the way out in Quetzaltenango or Totonicapán. I could be trusted to deliver, to not sell customers' expensive items from the States to other customers and claim they had gone missing. And I had fair prices; I charged by the pound once the laundry had been pressed and folded, not when it was wet, like many of the other places in the surrounding areas. But there was still something to be said for speediness, even in a slow-moving place like ours.

"Put it on the counter," I said when I noticed the girl still holding a basket, like she was scared to set it down.

"Go get me the iron," I said, telling her where to find it. I pulled the ironing board out of the closet, then took the iron from the girl, filled it with water, and plugged it in. While we waited for it to get hot, I finally asked her name.

"Gloria," she said. "Like, to God."

I nodded. "Very good," I said.

"¿You?"

"Amadeo," I said. "As in, lover of."

She looked at the ground. "¿Ever feel like you don't live up to your name?" She kicked at some dirt she'd dragged in on her shoes right as the iron began to hiss.

I turned to it, ignoring her question. "¿Do you know how to use this?" I asked. She nodded uncertainly. "Come here," I said, then pulled out one of the bedsheets from the nearest basket. "Normally," I said, "we have to keep all the orders separate so nothing goes home with the wrong customer." I signaled at the baskets. "Luckily, these all belong to the hotel, except for those two." I pointed at the two baskets of clothes; one belonged to Emiliano, who owned the bakery in town, and the other belonged to Ricardos, one of the city's workers who dug holes in the jungle and filled in the ones on the highway; almost every article of clothing belonging to him had tears in it, including his underwear, so there was no getting the two mixed up.

I was showing Gloria how to iron sections when there was a knock on the door. I opened it to find Magdalena standing under a blue tarp she was using to keep dry.

"¿Is she here?" she asked. I told her she was and asked Magdalena to come inside. "I would have brought her myself, but Manuelito's not feeling well and I didn't want to leave him until his dad got back from work," Magdalena said, shivering at the door.

"Let me get you some tea," I said.

"I'm okay," Magdalena said. "I'm glad she found you."

I nodded. "¿Who is she?" I dug the note from my pocket and handed it to her to read to me.

She didn't take it, had already read it. "Someone who needs help," Magdalena said.

"¿Why can't you take her to the church?" I asked, pocketing the note.

Magdalena let out a small sigh, then looked around me to see if Gloria was nearby.

"She's in the living room," I said.

Magdalena nodded. "She can't go back to the church," Magdalena said, explaining the situation. Gloria had been taken to a nunnery by her parents after they'd come home one day to find a boy in her room. The mom said she'd been like that for as long as she could remember: always one eye on the priest at church and the other on a boy. The dad added that he was sure she'd find a way to watch those young men even while her eyes were closed in prayer. But it wasn't just that. She refused to do her schoolwork or help with chores at home. She was picking fights and started pulling her hair out in clumps. They'd taken her to the nunnery thinking the sisters could help, but she'd gotten kicked out when the nuns found out she was pregnant. She'd been there for two months, and they never noticed any blood on her underwear when they washed her clothes. It was against the rules—they couldn't have a pregnant ward or novice—but when they tried to give her back to her parents, her parents wouldn't take her.

"Her *tíos* brought her here because it's far from their town. They left her by the highway with that note and a few hundred *quetzales*," Magdalena finished, shivering even harder, but not from the cold this time.

"¿But why bring her here?" I asked, signaling at my walls.

Magdalena took a step toward me, and it took all my willpower and some strength from above not to take a step back. "Because you're trying to make up for something," she said. "This is your chance."

Before I could respond, I heard a scream that shook the inside of my bones. Then I heard something breaking on the floor. Magdalena and I rushed into the living room, and there was Gloria, holding her hand to her chest, then bringing it up to her lips and blowing on it. She waved it in the air, then put four fingers in her mouth. Tears were forming at the corners of her eyes.

Magdalena rushed over. "¿What happened?" she said, taking Gloria's hand in her own.

"I tried to catch it," she said. She'd bumped into the ironing board and tried to save the iron from falling.

"Come," Magdalena said, leading Gloria to the bathroom in the back and turning on the tap.

I began picking up the pieces of the iron. It was broken, but not beyond repair. I unplugged it from the wall and set it back on the ironing board. The soleplate was lying on the ground, but I knew it was too hot to pick up yet. I looked at the sheet Gloria had been working on, expecting it to be burnt. But it wasn't. It was as white as could be, and I ran my hand along the fabric— still warm, without a single wrinkle anywhere.

THE NEXT DAY, I took the iron to Felipe to have him look at it. The fix was simple enough. A screw here, a spring there, and it was good as new.

"¿How much do I owe you?" I asked, but Felipe shook his head and waved his hand in my face like my money wasn't good there. I thanked him. "Next load's on me," I said, then watched as Felipe said goodbye to Gloria like she'd been there her whole life. It was no surprise that the whole town knew about her already. In a place like that, where nothing ever happened, even a stray dog passing through was news. I said goodbye, and when Felipe turned to walk to the back of his shop, I left the money I owed him on the counter.

Gloria and I stopped by the *mercado* for eggs, *frijoles*, fresh tortillas, and a few things she said she liked—TorTrix, *agua de jamaica*—then began the walk back home. She was eating a prepackaged ice cream I'd bought her, asking if I was sure I didn't want her to pay me back for it. "I have some money," she said, but I told her it was fine. That it was best she keep it, just in case. She didn't push the issue, just licked at one of the trails of melting ice cream sliding down her burnt hand, like a wild animal tending a wound.

"I won't stay forever," she said, licking at another trail.

"Okay," I said. We passed a few kids sitting on a stoop playing jacks.

"¿Did they bring me to you because you don't have any?" she asked, nodding toward the children.

"Possibly," I said. I didn't tell her that I did have a child once, that his name was Milagro, and that he'd be grown by now, eighteen, maybe nineteen.

"¿You didn't want them?" she asked.

I turned to watch her. Who did this little girl think herself to be, asking such personal questions? She'd made me angry, and before I could stop them, the words came flying out of my mouth. "Just like your parents didn't want you," I said. Not even my closest friends in town—granted, there weren't many, and we were mostly friends simply because we played dominoes on the weekends—not even *they* knew about my son, nor had they ever been rude enough to ask. So yes, maybe I wanted to be cruel, to teach her a lesson, but already I worried I'd gone too far.

"I'm sorry," I said, but she acted like she hadn't heard me say anything.

We stayed silent for the rest of the walk, and I thought about my son. I remembered the day we'd lost him. He'd been almost seven when my wife, Alma, had taken him to the weekend market in Esquipulas, the town closest to us then. She'd been pregnant with our second child, and all I'd done during the pregnancy was complain about how worried I was about money.

"The child comes always with a loaf of bread under its arm," my parents used to say, but I hadn't found that to be the case, and now I was going to have another. I worked selling small toys, peanuts, and mangoes along the highway and relied on people driving by to stop and purchase something. Sometimes they did, but usually, even if I stood next to the speed bumps, where cars had to slow down, they would just drive off.

My wife and son were in Esquipulas when a taxi carrying two foreigners hit Alma. She said they hit her so hard that her *chanclas* flew off her feet. Milagro must have been standing on the curb, distracted by something—a new toy a street vendor was hawking, a game of checkers between two old men, or maybe a mangy dog biting at its paws. He was always like that, watching the butterflies instead of helping me peddle goods to cars or bringing up buckets of water with his mom like all the other children in town. Alma said she woke up in the hospital and the first thing she asked for was Milagro. She said the doctor had chuckled and said that the taxi hadn't hit her that hard. "The strike to the head when you hit the ground is what knocked you out," he said, adding that the real miracle was that the tourists coughed up the money for the bill. "You'll be a little sore, but you'll be fine," he said.

Alma explained that Milagro was our son, that he'd been with her at the market. The doctor checked the notes on her chart and said, "It says here you came in alone."

Alma tried to get up but got dizzy. She looked out the window; the sun was setting. "I need to find him," she said.

When she was able to stand without assistance—a few minutes later, she said—she'd gone back to the market, but the stalls were closed for the night. She'd walked all of Esquipulas calling Milagro's name. When the last bus up the mountain was scheduled to leave, she'd boarded it, thinking that maybe he'd found his way home, that maybe someone had given him the fare.

When she got back, I was waiting, wondering what was taking them so long. Dinner was going and I called to them from the kitchen, but when I turned around, I saw that her head was wrapped in a bandage and that Milagro was not by her side. I rushed to her, expecting something bad to have happened, but what had happened was much worse than what I could have ever imagined. When she told me, I toppled chairs, broke dishes, threw furniture, and, worst of all, I yelled at Alma, blamed her for what had happened. Finally, I cursed myself for not having shown Milagro how to get back home from the market, from Honduras, from the moon—from anywhere he needed to.

I walked to that market every day for almost a year, even during the months it wasn't open, and waited for hours on end, but Milagro never came back. And the other child never came. A few days after the car had hit her, Alma started to bleed, and the baby had to be taken out of her. Unable to deal with the pain, I left. Found a place as far away from there as I could and began washing clothes for one of the places with the fancy dryers all the way in Quizabal, hundreds of kilometers away.

Not long after, I moved to Quetzaltepan and started hand-washing clothes.

I was putting away the last of the items we'd gotten at the market while Gloria stood in the living room, finishing her ice cream. I cracked my knuckles, feeling as though I should say something else to her, to try to make up for what I'd said to her about her parents on the walk, but I was scared to make it worse. I was reaching for words when there was a knock on the door. I knew it was another load of clothes, and abandoned the idea of saying anything else to Gloria.

When I walked back in holding the basket, Gloria was watching me from the couch. "¿Do you want to help me?" I asked. She followed me to the stone basin out back and watched as I filled it with soap and warm water. Then I pulled out the first piece of laundry—a nightgown—and showed her how to scrub the fabric against itself so that it didn't agitate and wear down the threads but still hard enough to remove all the smells and stains. When I finished, I held the nightgown up for her to inspect it. "Just like new," I said, then reached in for the next article of clothing.

THE FOLLOWING DAY, Omar, the baker, knocked on my door while Gloria and I were finishing up a load.

He was sorry for disturbing me and taking up my time. He knew I was busy, what with the new addition to the household and everything, but he was missing one of his aprons and wondered if I had seen it.

I told him I hadn't but that I would ask Gloria. He thanked me, said he had to get back to the bakery, that it wasn't a problem, but that if I found it, he wanted it back;

otherwise, it was fine. I promised him I would look for it. "If it's here," I said, "I'll find it." I closed the door and walked out back, where Gloria was hanging clothes to dry.

"We're missing an apron," I said. Omar rotated three aprons per load and I remembered folding all three the day Gloria had burned herself. Or at least I thought I had. There were other things on my mind then, such as finding Gloria a bed for her room, which the church had ultimately agreed to give me and brought over that night in the rain, the mattress covered in a tarp to keep it dry, and cleaning out the room, full of nothing but spiderwebs and dust. I'd never utilized that bedroom—I barely occupied my own—and was glad to be putting it to use.

"¿What's it look like?" Gloria asked, scanning the piles of clothes.

"It's not there," I said. "But keep an eye out for it."

She nodded, then brought the basket inside. I walked to the cupboard where I kept the iron, but it wasn't in there, so I reached farther back, as if there were a secret opening.

"I have it in my room," Gloria said. She walked to the back of the house and returned holding it.

"¿Why was it back there?" I asked.

"I was practicing," she said, and I believed her.

That weekend, two of the local women stopped by. One was missing a skirt and the other a shawl. I couldn't understand where the clothes were going, and though I didn't know it at the time, there was talk in town that Gloria was stealing items and selling them so she could afford a ticket to somewhere else or so she could get an abortion. People shook their heads.

I hadn't heard any of the rumors until the weekly domino game at Hector's house. Patricio, who normally didn't say much, brought it up.

"¿Who would she be selling it to?" I asked. She had no transportation, and other than when we were asleep or I was at Hector's, she was with me at all times of the day.

"I'm just saying," Patricio said, "if she could get pregnant without her parents finding out, ¿what else could she be doing?"

I'd heard enough. Slammed my dominoes on the table and left.

"Just think about it," Hector called after me, but I kept walking.

As the weeks went by, more and more of the townspeople stopped bringing their clothes. I'd run into them at the café or in the street and they would sneer or make a show of checking their pockets for their wallets or spare change. The men would say things like, "Looks like I managed to keep my socks" and laugh. Pretty soon, the kids were imitating their parents, saying, "Put your jerseys back on" when they saw me coming down the road. They'd pause their soccer game and rush to the sidewalk and laugh. "Oh no, Angel forgot his tank top," they'd say, and Angel would rush back to grab it before I got any closer.

Finally, when Magdalena came by about a month after Gloria showed up, looking for a pair of her underwear, the expensive one her husband had gotten her for her birthday, I decided I needed to do something about the situation. I'd given Gloria the benefit of the doubt, had ignored the signs, but it was getting to be too much; we needed money, and I needed my reputation back.

"¿Why don't you go buy us more soap?" I said to Gloria, handing her some money.

"¿By myself?" she asked. She was dressed in new clothes— ones I'd bought her a few days after she'd moved in, a few sizes too big for when the baby began to need more room—and there were no new bald spots on her head.

"I need to stay here and start the next load," I said.

She took the money from me and stuffed it in her bra—something we'd also gone to get her. The moment she left, I walked to her room. Until I had cleaned it out for Gloria, I hadn't been inside since the day I moved into the house, and I had not been in the room again since it had become Gloria's. I stood with my hand on the door handle and hesitated before opening the door, knowing I was violating her trust.

I walked in and checked her closet. Nothing but the outfits I'd gotten her, and the iron. I took it out and set it aside; I didn't understand why she kept moving it into her room since it wasn't like we did any ironing in there. I checked under her bed, but there was nothing there either. Where could she be hiding the missing items? I started to think I'd been wrong, that the whole town had been wrong, that they'd simply misplaced their own things. I looked at her bed again, and suddenly I couldn't remember if we'd ever cleaned the sheets the church had given us, so I decided to wash them as an apology, as a justification for why I'd been in her room. I began to strip the bed.

When I reached the mattress, I noticed that it had misshapen lumps I hadn't seen the day it was delivered. I pushed on one and it didn't resist the way a spring should, looked like the hump on a camel. I pushed on another and saw a thread coming loose in the seam of the diamond pattern of the mattress. I pulled on the thread and it came undone easily. Pretty soon, I'd opened the tear wide enough so that my hand would fit in the hole. And when I reached in, I pulled out a pair of socks and a child's onesie. Then I made another hole and pulled out the shawl and Magdalena's underwear. I kept pulling on the seams Gloria had sewn shut until I ran out. Some of the articles had pieces missing, torn away—shirts with the sleeves gone, pants with a missing leg—and some were discolored with stains she hadn't been able to fully get out, but some of them were unharmed: the onesie, bibs, cloth diapers. I reached back in, and when I pulled out Omar's apron and Maria's skirt, I was convinced I hadn't yet found everything. I went into the kitchen and grabbed a knife. I stabbed at the mattress and pulled out handful after handful of stuffing, scattering it all around the room. I kept going until I reached the bedsprings but couldn't stop. I tore and tore, panting, my hands aching from the strain, until the mattress was unrecognizable.

Finally, completely out of breath, shoulders aching as though I'd been washing clothes for the better part of a year without stopping, I pulled out from the last piece of foam a pair of the underwear I'd bought Gloria the day we went shopping for clothes. I held them in my hand. There in the center of the fabric was a faded red stain.

That's when I remembered the night a little over two weeks before when I'd woken up to get a glass of water and had seen Gloria's door open. I'd heard the sound of water splashing and walked out back, where Gloria was standing in her white nightgown, hands deep in the basin, scrubbing, not the way I'd taught her, but viciously, like she was trying to get rid of something.

"¿What are you doing?" I'd asked. And she'd let out a little yelp, like a dog when you accidentally step on its tail, and turned to look at me.

"¿Why are you awake?" she said. She looked over her shoulder at the basin, and we watched as water dripped down the side, making plopping sound as it hit the ground. "I'm getting a head start on tomorrow," she said, turning back to face me.

I'd told her I admired her dedication but that we needed our rest, and the clothes wouldn't dry at night. "Go to bed," I said, and she said she would. Then I'd gotten my glass of water and walked by her still standing there in the roofless courtyard.

This is what she'd been hiding: her period.

"¿What are you doing?" It was Gloria. She was standing in the doorway to her room holding the soap I'd sent her out to buy.

"¿What's this?" I said, holding the evidence out to her.

"That's private," she said, dropping the soap, then running into the room and snatching her underwear from me. When the bottle of soap hit the floor, the cap flew off and the soap began to spill everywhere.

"¿You think we're washing the floors?" I said, rushing over to pick it up.

"¿What did you do to the bed?" she yelled.

I held the bottle, soap leaking onto my shoes. "¿Why were you hiding that from me?" I yelled back.

She looked indignant. "I'm leaving," she said, then went into the closet and started pulling clothes off the hangers.

I was scared she meant it, but all I could think to say was "¿To go where?" I followed her as she went to the kitchen, pulled a trash bag from under the sink, and returned to her room. "You don't have anybody," I said as I watched her throw clothes into the bag. "No one wants you."

She stopped filling the trash bag and turned to me. I thought she was going to start screaming again, but instead, she punched the soap bottle out of my hand. She turned back to her clothes and reached for a shirt, fingers lingering on the fabric.

She began crying. And all of a sudden, I was back in that house with Alma after she'd told me what had happened to Milagro. I looked around at the mess I'd made, all the destruction I was causing.

I wanted to apologize but couldn't find the words, and settled for reaching out my dry, arthritic hand and placing it on Gloria's shoulder as it jerked from her sobbing. At my touch, she flinched and moved from under the weight of my arm. I didn't know what else to do. I thought she'd moved because she'd made up her mind and there was no changing it now. But instead, Gloria turned to face me and began to pull off her shirt.

"¿What are you doing?" I said, averting my eyes.

"It's not like that," she said, then stood still until I looked at her, standing in her bra, searching my eyes like she was looking for an answer to a question she'd been asking herself. I looked at her body, and I almost couldn't believe what I was seeing. Yes, I had figured out she wasn't pregnant, so I wasn't surprised when I laid eyes on her flat stomach. Instead, I was shocked by all the burns. She had small ones, the size of the tip of the iron, and slightly larger ones, like the one on the shoulder I'd just touched, which was still fresh. That's when I looked more closely at the clothing items I'd pulled out of the mattress, the ones with the missing pieces and the stains. She'd been using some of the clothes to bandage the fresh burns she'd been giving herself.

"I hid my bloody underwear from the nuns so they'd kick me out," she said. She was looking at the ground then, no longer making eye contact with me, letting me take in the full extent of her burns. "I hid it from you so you'd keep me."

It was my turn to cry. Looking at her, at how she was punishing herself, I couldn't bear it. My eyes were closed, and I had my arms crossed across my chest, but I felt her take them and put them around her body and felt her head on my chest.

"Let it out," she said, and I did. I cried until I was sure our clothes were soaked through, until I was sure I'd shed enough tears to fill up the basin out back.

When I stopped, she took me by the hand and led me to the courtyard, where the latest batch of laundry—the hotel's bed linens—hung on the clothesline. A storm was rolling in again, and the sky was growing dark.

"Help me," she said, then began taking down the sheets, but she wasn't moving them to the baskets or bags, she was letting them fall to the ground, and I understood. We took down all the sheets, every shirt, every sock, and left them scattered around us. If someone were to have looked down from the sky, they would have thought we'd roped down the clouds. When we were done, we sat in all that whiteness as the wind blew dirt across the newly washed surfaces. We waited for the rain to begin and didn't move, even when the mud began to form beneath us and the clouds on the ground turned the color of the storm-heavy ones in the sky.

Acknowledgments

This book wouldn't be in your hands if it wasn't for my agent, Eric Simonoff, who believed enough in my work to help find it a home. To my editors, Sara Birmingham and Gabriella Doob, thank you for helping each of these stories reach their full potentials; and to everyone else on the Ecco team who helped make this book come together—Sonya Cheuse (publicist of the year every year), Meghan Deans (fastest bookmark gunslinger in the West and executive marketing director extraordinaire), Helen Atsma for welcoming me to the Ecco team, Frieda Duggan for being the person behind the curtain pulling all of the strings that make proofing, scheduling, and copyediting possible, TJ Calhoun for keeping me on track to meet deadlines, Nina Leopold for making sure I got the window seat on my flights and for giving such detailed itineraries that even *I* couldn't mess things up, Miriam Parker for working around the clock to get me in front of readers and booksellers, and Vivian Rowe for the absolutely stunning and kickass artwork on the cover of this book.

Thank you to SIBA and NAIBA for having me at NVNR—my first time on a panel talking about this book—and to the wonderful HarperCollins book sales reps I met while there—Ronnie, Onyew, Ian, and Kim—thank y'all for accepting me into your group with open arms, drinks in hand.

Thank you to everyone who believed enough in this book to promote it, including Cebo Campbell, John Manuel Arias, Ruben Reyes Jr., Melissa Lozada-Oliva, Jess Walter, Cristina Henríquez, Santiago Jose Sanchez, and Javier Zamora; I will forever be indebted to your kindness, support, and thoughtful words.

To Jeff Condran, the first person to ever believe in me as a writer even when I showed up to undergraduate classes hungover and smelling of cigarettes, I wouldn't be here if it wasn't for you and your continued guidance.

To my good friends—too many of you to list, but you know who you are—for keeping me sane while I worked on these stories.

To Taylor, Jack, and Felix—I'm sorry I've spent so much time locked in my office working on these books. I hope you will forgive me and see that this is all for you.

Lastly, to the people of Guatemala—those whom I knew growing up, those whom I met during my travels back to the country of our ancestors, and those whom I didn't meet—you all made this book possible in a million different ways.